For Con and Rachel,
when the evenings are dark
and the nights long.

'The people that walked in darkness
has seen a great light;
on those who live in a land of deep shadow
a light has shone.'

Isaiah 9:1

LAND of DEEP SHADOW

Pat Hynes

WOLFHOUND PRESS

First published 1993 by
WOLFHOUND PRESS
68 Mountjoy Square
Dublin 1

Wolfhound Press receives financial assistance from the Arts Council / An Chomhairle Ealaíon, Dublin, Ireland.

British Library Cataloguing in Publication Data
Hynes, Pat
Land of Deep Shadow
I. Title
823.914 [J]

ISBN 0-86327-344-0

Cover design: Jan de Fouw
Cover and text illustration: Jane Doran
Typesetting: Wolfhound Press
Printed by the Guernsey Press Co Ltd, Guernsey, Channel Isles

The Beginning

Find a lonely spot, very late on a star strewn night, or early on a misty morning. Camouflage yourself well; wait and watch. If you are very lucky you will see one of the strangest sights in the animal kingdom, a hares' parliament.

The hares all gather, silently, and sit, quite still and erect, in a circle. Then, one of the older hares will begin to tell a tale, some singular story from long, long ago. The younger ones will listen carefully, committing it to memory for when it will be their turn to recite.

And if the moon is full and the wind the merest whisper, one of the hares might recite from the most fabled of all epic tales, 'The Prophecy of Tuarug'. Its origins are as shrouded in mystery as its meaning. Indeed, much of it has been lost and only remnants now remain. These remnants are only recited when a special spirit is present. Thus the great tale is passed on and remembered by the few who are charged with its transmission from one generation to the next.

What follows here is not 'The Prophecy of Tuarug'. Such an undertaking is not possible. Rather it is a story, in which much licence is used, based upon the scant information available. The story itself is as much a quest as was, perhaps, the original prophecy. It is a quest for that which remains hidden from most of us but for which a deep and profound yearning is always felt. It is the quest for the meaning of our existence.

'. . . every generation throws up a so-called freak, one who is not content with the normal, run-of-the-mill life of a hare. Such a one will be special because he will be attentive to that which is not easily discerned. His life will seem to be a contradiction. He will not be content to wander aimlessly, rather he will seek a purpose.
'That purpose will be made known to him and, if he is truly a "Seer", he will respond . . .'

Prophecy of Tuarug 1 : 8-9

PART ONE: The Stirring

Chapter One

The roaming rain-laden clouds scurrying across the sky; the wind, moaning and weaving through the grasses; the darkness and silence hanging heavily on the night; and the solitude, deep and mystical; these were his earliest memories. Perhaps they were the impressions engrained in every hare's early consciousness. Packo did not know. Certainly they constituted his own.

Then, of course, there were the daily visitations of his mother. She would appear, huge, comforting, and warm. He would suckle and nuzzle against her, safe in her presence, wanting her to stay. She would speak gently, 'Packo, Packo, you're different, so unlike your brother and sister. Whatever will become of you?' The words meant little to him. Only her presence was special, and the loneliness he felt when she left was allayed only when she reappeared.

'Stay still my little one,' she would advise, 'stay still. We have many enemies and our defences are our extremes, our ability to blend perfectly into our surroundings, and our great speed. Wisdom is in their use.'

As he grew and felt the strength flourishing within him he would spend his solitude pondering her words. Why was being able to stay still a gift? It came naturally to him. Something inside, some instinct told him to sit still, to adopt a certain posture and remain relaxed for long periods. As for speed he had no experience. His powerful hind legs were well developed, but what was speed? Perhaps it was to move as fast as a strong wind, to become a part of it. Was that something only hares could achieve?

And then he wondered about his mother. Why did she only visit for such brief interludes? His brother and sister, where were they? How did he come to be here in this hollow, hidden from view by the long grasses? And why was he different? Had he been outcast, ostracised, removed from his kin because he was strange? What was the meaning of all this?

The questions remained locked in his head, a puzzling array of confusion, Then, one night, as his mother approached, he knew somehow that it was to be her last visit. He sensed, incomprehensibly, her sadness. He had spent much of the day nibbling at long stalks of grass, their juicy chewiness pleasant now that his weaning was complete. All that day he had longed for his mother, wanting her reassurance, welcoming the warm glow of her love. He stood on his hind legs and watched her. She was working her way nimbly through tufts of grass, appearing and disappearing as she passed around some obstacle. She was only a few paces from him when she looked up for the first time and caught his eye.

'Packo,' she greeted him, 'sorry I'm a little later than usual.' She looked away sheepishly. She sensed that he knew that this was to be the parting of the ways.

Silence heralded their togetherness.

'I've come to say goodbye, Packo,' she said, finally.

'Yes, I know.'

Silence again.

'I know,' Packo began, 'but I don't understand.'

'Yes,' his mother nodded, her voice soft, gentle. 'Sometimes we know without understanding. Tonight Packo, I said goodbye to your brother and sister. They do not understand either, yet they know it is our way, the hare's way. They did not need to understand, they simply accepted. But you Packo, I've always sensed that when the time came you would want a reason, an explanation.'

Packo gazed at her quizzically. He felt the tears rushing to his eyes, realised that only emptiness lay before him.

'Let me try to explain, Packo, let me try to tell you how life is. You don't remember your brother and sister. You were all born at the same time. As soon as darkness fell I separated you. Yes, it was I who put you in this isolation. Three newly born leverets together tend to attract attention. Hawks and foxes and other predators prey upon us, so, for safety's sake, we separate our young. You see, we have two main methods of defence. We can remain motionless, or we can run and certainly no fox would be able to stay with us. Our reddish brown coats flecked with tawny gold and black blend us perfectly with the long grasses and we are camouflaged. Our sense of smell warns us of even the faintest foreign odour and prepares us for danger. Our lives are lived in continual peril and many of us do not survive to adulthood. So you see, there is reason in our strange ways. Your brother and sister, who are little more than a hundred bounds from here in different directions, understood all this instinctively. But you, Packo, you are different. They accept while you question. What is it about you, Packo?'

The question hung in the still air for several moments. She knew, as Packo knew, that he had no answer.

'And now, Packo,' she continued, 'I have to tell you that you have no further need of me. Oh! I'm not heartless. You've survived so far by chance. No predator has spotted you. Now you must begin to make your own way, and the way of the buck is to roam. It is to seek out a doe and win her. It is to mate and then continue on. Life as a hare is about survival, nothing more. You'll survive, Packo, you'll survive because you're special. You have a calling and a destiny. I don't know any more than that, I cannot explain. You are young and strong and the time has come for you to leave this place, this peace that belongs only to the very young. You must leave here and go, find your destiny. Know that in the quiet evening air, in the torrid midday heat, in the very heart of the greatest danger, I will be with you. A doe gives birth to many leverets in the course of her life but only once is she afforded the knowledge that one of her offspring is special.

You are special, Packo. I don't know how, or why, or what you must do. But believe me, out there, out in the great expanses, the very purpose of your life will come to fruition. Your challenge is to seek that purpose, I know no more. What I do know is, if you go to seek that challenge, if you throw yourself into exploration, your questions will be answered, your wanderings will have a purpose. Follow that purpose, Packo, wherever it might lead, follow it.'

She moved closer to him. A faint breeze moaned momentarily. He felt her wet snout very close to his and her forepaw run gently down the side of his head. There was a great sadness in her eyes, something more than the sadness of a mother bidding farewell to her son, a sadness which devoured and engulfed him.

And then she was gone, stealing stealthily into the night, blending with it as she had done so many times before.

Chapter Two

Packo sat silently for long moments after his mother's departure. Usually he listened to the strange noises of darkness; the scurrying of field mice, the languid hoot of the owl, the soft caress of a gentle breeze touching the grasses, the shattering pit-patting of the heaviest rain. Tonight he heard nothing save the constant beat of his heart. Tonight he could imagine himself being the only living creature trapped on a planet of death, of nothingness.

As darkness lifted and dawn approached he felt that he wanted to shout out, to challenge the emptiness. He knew that it would be futile. He was alone, imprisoned by his longing for companionship, for friendship, for one with whom he could dissipate his sense of desertion. Here, in this lonely form, his whole world since he had grown into consciousness, there was no one to whom he could turn. What was it, he wondered, that his mother meant when she had so often referred to him as 'different'? Were his feelings now indicative of that difference? And if they were, what was he to do?

A glimmer of hope. Perhaps salvation was to be found in action? Mentally he toyed with the notion. What was his problem? Loneliness, a feeling of desertion. What must he do? Move! It was as simple as that! Move! Move in which direction? Did it matter? The thought struck him that his brother and sister were out there somewhere. Were they as confused as he? Perhaps he might find them. He remembered that his mother had approached earlier head on. She had said that she had already bade farewell to his brother and sister. Perhaps if he struck out straight ahead he might find one of them. He felt that he had to try.

He stood on his hind legs and gazed out into the pale dawn. The land spread out before him for as far as he could see. He stepped forward and began to pick his way gingerly through the long grass. A tuft blocked his way. He hopped over it discovering the power in his hind legs. It was an exhilarating feeling, and he had hardly made any effort. He began to marvel at the power that was his to utilise. He wondered how fast he could run, and for how long; how quickly he could attain full speed, how long he could sustain it, and how quickly he could stop. He wanted to know how far he could see and how far his sense of smell could detect the various fragrances which assaulted him as he moved forward. He wanted to investigate everything. Suddenly, the world had become an exciting place.

A squeal brought him to. He stopped and pricked his ears. He heard it again, quite audibly, to his left. Immediately he set course towards it and in a very short time came across a young doe. She was crouching in her form, eyes fearful, her snout twitching.

'Hello,' he said gently.

She looked up. Her split upper lip quivered.

Packo realised that this must be his sister.

'Did mother say goodbye to you too?' he asked.

She nodded.

'I'm Packo, what's your name?'

'Dersall,' she piped nervously.

'Well, Dersall, you've nothing to worry about. Not long ago I was shaking in my form just like you are now. But you know, I've suddenly discovered that the world is not such a bad place. I've begun my journey of discovery, it's quite a thrill, believe me.'

Packo hoped that his words would comfort her. She simply stared back blankly. She held her head askance. 'Where did you learn all those words?' she asked, 'what do they mean?'

'Mother used to speak to me. I suppose I learned from her. Didn't she speak to you?'

'She fed me, made me feel safe, that's all. There's something funny about you.'

The remark was full of young innocence, and all the more pertinent because of that. It was Packo's turn to lack understanding. His mother had always said that he was different, now his sister was reasserting that. What did they mean? He appeared much the same as she; the same colour fur, smooth and glossy; the same long ears, the same snout. He was slightly heavier but that was hardly a significant difference.

She hopped forward, then stood on her hind legs, ears pricked. Suddenly she sprang forward, ran several paces, and stopped. Then she laughed.

'Hey,' she shouted back to him, 'this is fun, come on.'

She turned and ran, leaping in the air with each pace, surprised by her energy. Packo ambled alongside her and smiled.

'This is terrific,' she giggled, 'I've been still for so long. I never imagined that I could do this.'

She raced forward and then leapt. She felt the air against her snout, the freedom of brief flight. As soon as she landed she dashed off once again, running hard, head low. After a hundred paces she stopped, sat up, and turned to see Packo just a step behind her.

'Wow, we can really shift, can't we?'

Her enthusiasm was infectious and Packo, forgetting her remarks about his strangeness, laughed with her.

'Race you to that large tree,' he suggested, pointing one of his forepaws in the direction of a huge oak. Without reply she was away, stealing a yard on him. Packo moved after her building up his momentum until he felt that he must be at maximum speed, the power pumping through his legs, the wind streaming past him as he automatically tucked in his head. The oak was still some distance away when he came alongside her. He steadied himself and adjusted his speed. He felt no desire to show off his greater strength.

They came to rest at the massive trunk. Dersall's lungs were gasping for breath. She didn't realise that pace is usually more important than speed.

'Take a breather,' Packo advised, 'you'll soon recover.' He moved around the base of the tree to survey the land. He was out of sight when he heard the sharp, shrill scream. He turned immediately without a thought of any danger to himself and was back to where he had left his sister seconds before. In front of him, barely six feet from the ground, he saw the hawk, wings flapping furiously, talons clinging tenaciously to Dersall's limp body. He charged forward, quick as a flash, and jumped, pushing himself off the ground with every ounce of energy he could muster. It would be a long time before he would jump as high again. He caught the back of his sister's body with his forepaws, surprising the hawk which had taken for granted that he was safe once airborne. The extra weight prized the talons apart and Dersall's body fell to the ground, blood oozing from both flanks. The hawk, unable to comprehend what had happened, rose high into the sky.

Packo dragged the broken body into a clump of grass and lay over it. He remained absolutely still. Only his eyes moved, rotating in their sockets, watching the skies for the return of their enemy. And then he spotted him, hovering high overhead, wings held steady, their tips pointing fractionally earthwards. The curved beak thrust down, betraying his menace. He was minutely searching the ground. Packo was naturally camouflaged and he had found thick grass in which to lie. A few paces to his rear even thicker, coarser grass beckoned. He knew that to move would court disaster. 'Lie still my little one, lie still.' His mother's advice rang clearly in his head. He resisted all temptation to seek greater security. As he scanned the skies he dared hardly to blink.

The hawk hovered for several moments, changing position occasionally in his close scrutiny of the ground. Then he disappeared from view. Packo rotated his eyes nervously. There was no sign of him. Packo remained perfectly calm. He realised that either the hawk had departed the scene or, and his blood chilled at the prospect, he was directly overhead filling the blind spot into which it was impossible to look without a very slight tilt of the head. He lay rigid, inert, fighting to control his growing fear.

Then, just beyond his place of concealment, the grasses moved. Was this a new danger come to confront him? Fear screamed at him, 'Run, run like the wind'. He remained steadfast. Suddenly he heard the flutter of flapping wings, felt the air disturbed. Despite their proximity he did not flinch. With magnificent self control he remained as still as ever. He was surrounded by the deafening beating of wings and the feather tips almost touched him. The hawk's gurgle of delight was so near that Packo thought he must break free. Those seconds of tension were like a lifetime of indecision. Had he taken the wrong course of action? Was his fate to be plucked from the ground, an easy prey to an easy slaughter? His rigidity became spell-like, he was petrified, quite unable to move. A small, pitiful squeal invaded his racing mind and there, not a pace in front of him, the flashing talons dug into a tiny fieldmouse, breaking its back like the storm wind breaks the bough. The predator rose, content, forgetting his earlier prey.

Packo was trembling. He scanned the skies. The hawk had gone, seeking solitude to enjoy the warm flesh of his kill. Packo stepped gently aside from Dersall's broken body. He ran his left forepaw over her head and placed his snout next to hers. He held his breath and stayed close for several seconds. He knew then that his worst fear was realised. Dersall was dead. For the first time he faced death. Why did one so young have to die? There was so much that he did not understand, but there was one thing he was clear about: he was angry.

The sky was overcast now, ponderous rain clouds had slowly rumbled across the heavens. Rhythmically, great drops of rain began to fall. At first they were eagerly absorbed into the dry ground. As the drops of rain became more frequent, puddles formed, huge black pools growing visibly as the clouds released their burden.

Packko stood motionless. The rain ran off him, stinging his eyes. It smashed into him, trying to subjugate him, to drive him down. He remained defiant as his spirit hardened and his anger began to find an outlet. Yes, he would survive. He would not lie down.

He stared at the limp body of his sister. She had been a loser. He would win. He had cast emotion from his heart. Oh, he was different all right. This death had taught him a great lesson; forget them all, seek your own salvation, never rely on anyone.

Dersall's flaccid body lay before him. The blood had congealed along her flanks, her mouth hung half open, her eyes stared into infinity. Briefly something tugged at his conscience. The inner voice told him that he should not leave her this way, that he should cover her, lay her to rest. The tugging was short lived. His anger shot through and without a further thought he turned and walked away.

The rain continued to lash him but he was oblivious to it. He was caught in a cocoon which shielded him from the outside world. He forgot even the most basic instinctive thoughts of safety. He didn't care. He trudged the open countryside. Eventually he began to trot, attempting to distance himself even further from that terrible place where he had witnessed death for the first time. How long he trotted or how far, he had no idea. He changed direction at random without observing any landmarks. He was going nowhere. Yet, he felt a strange strength within him, felt that no danger would come to him. The rain eased, the sky brightened from the west. He sought out a hollow surrounded by thick grass, wriggled in without disturbing it, and fell asleep.

When he awoke the sun was already low in the western sky, reddening the distant horizon, bathing it in soft colour and a sense of unreality. Packo stood on his four paws and stretched, arching his body before extending his legs to their extremities. He picked at a few blades of grass and munched them silently. As he stepped out of the clump of grass he discovered a patch of mushrooms which had sprung up after the rain and sun. He bit into one, savouring its taste and soft texture. There were several scattered about in clusters. He ate them greedily, welcoming his good fortune in their discovery.

As he finished his meal he noticed the slight chill in the air. The seasons were beginning to turn. The evenings were cooler now than the early days he had spent in his maternal form. The grasses were no longer charged with life but appeared to be taking on a withered look. Their zenith had passed. He wondered what it might mean.

Chapter Three

Packo's first winter was hard and bitter. He found himself flung against the elements, and he barely survived. When the snow first began to fall he was filled with wonder. He raced about, trying to catch the great flakes in his mouth, fascinated as they melted on his tongue. But the snow continued to fall and soon ceased to melt. He sought refuge in a hollow and pulled dead, languid grass around him. When he awoke several hours later his nightmare woke with him. He was buried in a great cold blanket. Frantically he kicked and pushed the snow away. His heart was pounding, his tension fever-pitched as he emerged. He gazed about, dumbstruck. For as far as he could see in any direction the earth was shrouded in white. Even the trees, long since leafless, had changed colour. The blinding landscape made his eyes water. And it was cold, so very, very, cold.

The snow soon ceased to be soft, something he could jump through and frolic in. It became hard, razor-edged, forbidding. The frozen wastes became lifeless, devoid of comfort. Food became scarce and to conserve energy he sat for long hours huddled in a freezing form he had scraped out. Occasionally he found dead grass which he chewed eagerly. He reingested his droppings to satisfy his hunger.

After several nights of snow and freezing temperatures, he realised that there were two options open to him. He could continue to sit the weather out, and hope for a thaw, or he could go in search of food. If he remained where he was, he might starve to death, unless the cold took him first. If he wandered out in the open, he would be at risk, not only from the elements, but from predators who were themselves searching for food.

He stood and surveyed the great white expanse which filled his vision. He screamed at it, an anguished and tormented scream. His defiance was a slim lifeline. It sustained his anger, an anger directed against the unknown. Packo stepped arrogantly from his form. A north easterly wind bit into him, a chilling reminder that the death-life struggle was all around him. He put his head down and began to lope over the crisp land. The uppermost snow layer was frozen and his paws left hardly an impression upon it. Eventually he reached a hedgerow into which he crawled. In its centre, amidst the thick hawthorn growth, he found a few tasteless blades of grass which he chewed lethargically. He rested for a while until once more he felt the cold seeping into his body. He had to move on.

He began to lope again, keeping his body low, his centre of gravity as close to the ground as possible in an effort to avoid breaking through the topmost layer of snow which, strangely, appeared a little softer on this side of the hedge. The dull ache of hunger rendered him leaden and he forced himself to concentrate totally on his movements. He discovered that he could shut out the world around him, become enclosed in a cocoon, a cocoon of movement and speed. His powerful hind legs thrust him forward as he glided over the crisp white land. He breathed in shallow, even gasps, rhythmically striding on.

Suddenly the fields were green again, the sun was on his back and he was loping off to join other jacks in search of a doe, in search of excitement. Laughter was all around him. He spotted the doe. Her scent was strong and pungent, her gait graceful, her twitching snout acknowledging his presence. She eyed him momentarily, sufficient to issue an invitation that he should give chase. His heart charged within him, he was eager to court and win her. Yet, whereas he stood still she did not linger. She bounded forward, a different jack seeking her as the prize . . .

He came to and realised that he had been dreaming. He was

tired, so very tired. He glanced around. A hedge, over to his right. That would have to do. He pushed a way in and scraped out a shallow form. He cried out, a desperate, pitiful scream. Then he lay down and fell into a deep sleep. It was a voice that finally woke him.

'Take it easy, young fellow. You're alive, weak, but alive. You'll survive.'

'Who? What?'

An older hare raised his paw. 'All in good time, all in good time. Here, try to eat.'

The older hare pushed some dried grass towards him. It didn't look particularly appetising. Packo's face must have registered his lack of enthusiasm.

'Go on, taste it.' The older hare chuckled, his voice was warm and affectionate.

Packo gingerly nibbled at the grass and then looked up surprised.

'Hey, that's good,' he said, 'what is it?'

He didn't wait for a reply but eagerly chewed on finding that it contained hard pellets that greatly enhanced it.

'Grain,' the older hare replied. 'I always collect some in the autumn and store it for the hard times ahead!'

Packo hardly heard the words. He chewed and bit deeply, grinding the grain between his teeth, thoroughly enjoying the feast. He had forgotten what a full belly felt like. He glanced at the older hare and fell fast asleep!

He didn't know how long he had slept. When he awoke he was alone. He remembered the food that he had eaten and that he had spoken to someone. He felt stronger. In front of him was more of the dried grass he had eaten earlier. He nibbled at it and again found it satisfying. Then he heard a movement behind him. Instinctively he crouched in anticipation of attack.

'No need to worry, young fellow, it's only me.' The older hare appeared in his line of vision. Packo felt foolish.

'And there's no need to feel embarrassed either,' he added kindly as if he was able to read Packo's mind. 'Nature has made us all react to surprise in much the same way. It's a blessing we should all be grateful for, an innate gift very necessary for survival.'

'Who are you?' Packo asked bluntly, 'and what do you want with me?'

'The first question is easily answered if all you wish to know is my name.'

Packo's expression showed that he did not understand. The older hare noticed but made no attempt to explain.

'My name is Marsha. As to your second question, what do I want with you? Well, I merely heard your death cry. Similar cries I have heard all too often. I came to see if I could help, that's all.'

'Where am I?' Packo asked.

'In a small tunnel I dug out a few feet below the place I found you.'

Packo's eyes now registered surprise. 'A tunnel you dug out!' he said incredulously.

'Yes,' Marsha replied. 'You see, snow is cold to the touch and yet is also a great insulator, to protect us from the cold. When I found you, you were ready to die; you were cold, hungry, and dispirited. You had had enough. Your death cry told me that you were also angry. You were not really ready to die, but life had closed in around you and you saw no alternative. Well, I can make sure that you don't freeze to death or die of hunger. I can help restore you to physical health if you'll allow me, I'll help restore your spirit too. It's up to you.'

'How long did I sleep?'

'Oh, half a day the first time and then, after you had eaten your fill, a day and a night.'

'A day and a night,' Packo exclaimed, 'I didn't think it was possible for anyone to sleep for that long.'

Marsha chuckled. 'Oh yes, and I imagine that after you've eaten again you'll fall asleep for another long stretch. It's quite natural as your body returns to normal. The food is helping to restore your strength.'

'But I don't feel tired,' Packo objected.

'I'm sure you don't, but you do feel hungry?'

'Yes.'

'Right. Well I've brought more supplies of dried grass and grain, and a few hazel nuts.'

Marsha turned and pulled a bundle into the tunnel. It was neatly wrapped in a large leaf.

'I find these "dock" leaves invaluable. Put what you've got inside and tie it all up with a long strand of grass.'

He bit at the appropriate point and the leaf fell open disgorging dried grass mingled with grain and a number of hazel nuts.

'You must crack the outer shell like this,' Marsha advised him, 'to get to the core.' He took a nut between his teeth and it split apart as he exerted pressure on the shell. He offered the nut, which had lain hidden inside, to Packo. Packo crunched on it.

'Very tasty,' he said.

'Come then,' Marsha encouraged him. 'Eat. If you need a drink take a bite of snow, there's plenty of that.'

Packo began to eat. He moistened the food occasionally by taking a scoop of snow and sucking on it. He ate for some time while Marsha sat by silently, grinning. There was little left when Packo lifted his head and sat up. He felt contented and strangely warm. He yawned and his eyes began to close.

'You know, perhaps I will have a little nap.'

Marsha nodded and smiled.

Packo very quickly fell into a deep sleep. When he awoke Marsha was sitting in exactly the same position as before.

'Hi,' Packo greeted him.

'Hi yourself,' Marsha replied, 'How do you feel?'

'A little stiff! Better than I've felt for a long time. I'm sorry if I appeared to be rude earlier. I've been on my own for such a long time I was suspicious of you. Thank you for what you've done for me.'

'Oh, you don't have to apologise or thank me,' Marsha said. 'Really we should move from here. This is no more than a temporary shelter. If you'd like to tag along with me you'd be more than welcome.'

'I'd like that,' Packo told him.

'That's settled then. I'll take you to one of my permanent forms.'

'You have a permanent form?' Packo was astonished.

'First rule of survival, young fellow, always have a safe base.'

'By the way, my name is Packo,'

'Good, thank you for telling me. Now, come on Packo, follow me.' Marsha turned and trotted the short distance to the end of the tunnel. Packo followed and was immediately aware of the biting cold as he stepped out into the frosty night. He shivered and twitched his whiskers as the keen air met him. Marsha noticed his discomfort.

'You're not back to full strength yet, perhaps we should wait a little longer.'

'No, no,' Packo insisted, 'I'll be all right.'

'In this kind of weather there are only two options available to us. Either keep moving or find a warm place to rest. What we have to do now is keep moving. Stay on my heels, I know the safest way.'

Marsha headed into the endless frozen wastes, cantering for a little while to allow Packo to ease into the pace. As soon as he was satisfied that Packo's stiffness was wearing off he began to speed up. He loped forward, easily springing off his powerful hind legs with a minimum of effort. Packo was amazed at Marsha's stamina, surprised that the pace appeared to have no effect upon him. They had travelled some distance when Packo began to hurt. His lungs were not getting enough air, his legs were heavy, his head began to spin, and a nauseous sensation overtook him. Marsha was tuned in to his condition. 'Just a little further,' he urged, 'and then we can rest.'

They came to a hedgerow of intermingling holly and hawthorn. Marsha scooped aside some snow, enough to allow them entry into the thick heartland. Packo was breathing heavily while Marsha appeared to be quite comfortable.

'Aren't you even a little out of breath?' Packo struggled to ask.

'A little, yes. You must remember that you're still recovering from your ordeal, you're still weak. Also, you may never have given running much thought. When you were fit and healthy you took for granted that you could run quickly. With age we begin to learn the secrets of stamina and pace. We think about the posture that we adopt.'

'The secrets?' Packo asked, 'What are they?'

As was his wont Marsha chuckled. 'Well, firstly, always take short breaths through your mouth and not your snout. Secondly, keep your head low, there's less wind resistance that way and breathing is easier when you are travelling quickly. Thirdly build up your stamina, become knowledgeable in what your body can do. Practise your running.'

Packo was amazed. A hare practising running! Yet he could see the sense in the simple advice.

'And then there's pace,' Marsha continued. 'If possible try to run within your limits, that will enable you to remain in control. Panic is a hare's worst enemy. Should you need to extend yourself beyond your known limits, think ahead, never run blindly. You must be aware all the time that you must stop at some stage. Think, plan and consider where that stop will be. If you remain in control there's a better chance of finding a safe refuge. Remember too, sometimes it is wiser to run than to fight. Speed is one of our most important gifts. Intelligently used it is a powerful form of defence.'

Packo was stunned. He realised that he had much to learn and that fate had provided a teacher. He would be a willing pupil. But would Marsha accept him as such? 'Will you teach me?' Packo asked simply.

Marsha's eyes danced but his voice was grave. 'I will not be your teacher,' he replied, 'but I will be your friend.'

'My friend, what do you mean?'

'I'll tell you.'

Chapter Four

Marsha began his tale: —
The loud, raking explosion of the huntsman's horn and the ferocious baying of the hounds broke into the afternoon slumbers of two hares. Simultaneously they stood on their hind legs to peer above the grasses, and simultaneously both were spotted by the hounds who had already lost the fox's scent. The leader of the hunt saw the fresh prey; he decided to allow the hounds to give chase.

There was no time to think. Instinctively both hares sprang up and bounded away, attempting to put as much distance as possible between themselves and the bloodthirsty dogs. They ran quickly, rotating their eyes occasionally to glance behind. Approximately five hundred paces in front the hares spotted a copse. Both headed towards it. It would afford them height and, in amongst the thick elm and beech, an opportunity to take stock.

It was there that they hurriedly agreed their stategy which they hoped would provide them with the optimum chance of escape. Ahead of them, as the hilltop trees cleared, the undulating countryside unfolded into a patchwork of hedged fields. As the hounds approached, the hares ran into the open field, crouched and waited. The sniffing dogs made their way forward excited by the fresh scent. Suddenly, directly in front of the pack, the hares stood up. Then they split, each taking a different direction. Valuable seconds were gained as the dogs, hungry for the kill, were confused as to which hare to pursue. Then the dogs split, some taking after the hare to the right, others veering off to the left. Now the race began.

The hares charged across the open ground, the dogs chased in hot pursuit. The top of another rise presented itself and the hares, having each completed a semi-circular run, met at the highest point. They didn't stop to speak but criss-crossed each other's trail and continued to run down into the next set of fields.

When the two groups of hounds met, the mixed scents threw them into confusion. They yelped and sniffed and turned in circles. Then one picked up a fresh trail and howled excitedly. The others pricked their ears in recognition of the feverish call and they surged forward. The two hares were standing, a hundred yards apart, in the field below. The hare whose scent was discovered set off once more, racing in a great arc which would eventually take him to the top of the next rise. The other began a direct run to their next rendezvous where a derelict building marked a good vantage point from which to study the new ground beyond.

The hare who had been chased, the younger of the two, arrived well in front of the hounds. He breezed towards his companion, a smile across his face.

'I'm enjoying this. Listen, let's lead them back again, prolong the agony for them.'

'That would be foolish. We can easily escape now, why put ourselves at risk?'

The younger hare looked at his older companion. 'Haven't the neck for it eh! Well, I'll show you.'

He turned and ran swiftly down to meet the hounds. He cruised smoothly in a huge circle. He was happy. There was no way he could be caught. That old fogey had bottled out, obviously couldn't take the pace, didn't enjoy a bit of fun.

He was no more than ten paces from the brow of the hill when he caught sight of the black snouts and bared teeth of over thirty fresh hounds. He stopped in his tracks, disbelief in his eyes. He had left them all behind; where had these come from? The explanation was quickly revealed. The dogs who had given chase initially had not been the whole pack! The red coated-rider had kept some back! The hare realised that he had been foolhardy.

Then a blast of the horn tore the brief silence to shreds and the dogs charged. The hare turned immediately to run. The land was open and he was confident in his ability to escape.

Somewhere in the distance the horn shrilled again and he became aware of a column of hounds erupting from his left. The original pack had spotted him.

He accelerated to maximum speed. His motion was graceful, elegant, one of nature's fastest land creatures making full use of his strength. Suddenly, as his hind legs reached the ground once more, a searing pain shot through his body. He continued his surge, but with every bound he became increasingly aware of the acute discomfort in his right leg. He stopped momentarily and glanced hastily. A deep gash lacerated his paw, a clean, incisive cut welling blood. He tucked the leg beneath his body and continued on. He was beginning to tire. The dogs sniffed the blood and increased their pace. They knew that their prey was suffering.

The hare realised that they were gaining on him. Fear invaded his faltering steps. He tried to quicken his slackening pace but pain was shooting through his body. Behind the dogs bayed and howled and yelped. The fury of the entire pack was directed towards him.

There was some long grass ahead of him. He lurched into it, gasping for breath.

The older hare was waiting for him. 'Run up the slope to the deserted building. On the far side you'll find an old rabbit warren. Get in there and stay put. If any of the dogs follow you'll be quite safe. Wait for me there.'

The older hare stole forward and dashed at his foes. He kept his head low as he approached them and then, when he could no longer conceal himself, he burst at full speed between the two groups which had not quite met. He led them away from the younger hare back across the fields. He ran economically, knowing that once ahead his speed should bring safety. He kept an eager eye both behind and to the ground.

It was dusk when he finally strode up the hill. The ancient gable end of the building strutted upwards against the impending gloom, black against grey. The silence was total, eerie. The disused rabbit warren was behind the building. He made his way around the crumbling walks towards it. Then he heard the growls. Three dogs emerged from the undergrowth, surrounding him and pressing him against the wall. He was trapped.

Suddenly the dog to his left yelped loudly. His piteous cry transfixed the others. Above him, high up on the crumbling wall, the young hare stood erect. He had dislodged a huge piece of masonry and sent it hurtling on to the unlucky dog. The older hare leapt over the dog's body. As he moved the other two dogs sprang to life. The hare followed the boundary of the building. As the dogs scurried beneath him the younger hare pushed another huge and ancient boulder. It crashed down catching one of the two pursuers, severely wounding his left hind leg. He crawled off into the undergrowth. One dog left.

The hare jumped on to a low section of wall and nimbly gained height. Surely the dog would not follow. He did. Every step took him closer to the hare huddled at the far end.

Finally he stood barely a pace from the hare. He gloated, his eyes filled with hatred.

'Aroooo...'

The loud cry shattered the spell. It was issued from the other hare directly opposite. The dog turned his head. As he did so the trapped hare threw caution to the wind and, using his hind legs to push, jumped high. He leapt over the dog's head. The dog instinctively snapped at him, twisting awkwardly as he lost his footing. He toppled over, smashing into the ground below. He whimpered once and was quiet, his body broken.

The older hare landed safely and met the other in the centre of the wall. They hopped to the ground and trotted off at a brisk pace. Finally they climbed a hill where a thick copse would offer them shelter.

'Quite a day,' the younger hare said wearily.

'Indeed,' his companion replied.

'You saved me from my foolishness when you drew the dogs away. Thanks.'

'Yes, you saved my life too. Thanks.'

The youngster smiled. Suddenly he appreciated what a true friend was. But what gave him the greatest satisfaction was the fact that he had been a true friend himself. Now, that was special —

Chapter Five

Packo remained mesmerised by Marsha's eyes as the story ended.

'You were the younger hare,' he said, 'and there's more, isn't there?' Packo's voice was far away, living still in the images Marsha had so vividly created.

'Yes there is. I began to examine my life. I began to wonder why we are here. I sought solitude. I attempted to live my life deliberately, to strip the non-essentials away. What I discovered about myself was not pleasant. I had always imagined that mine was a carefree life; it was not so much carefree as careless. I had shied away from responsibility, always taking, never giving. I had never stopped to think.'

'That seems to be the way of the buck,' Packo prompted.

'Yes, but I began to feel that it was not good. To be so selfish is to court emptiness. I began to sense a presence. It seemed to me that some invisible force governs the world. I came to realise that everything happens for a purpose. Life is, at times, illogical. Yet, I do believe there is a plan, somewhere, somehow. And I believe that the plan is good. When I found you, Packo, you were about to die; you were angry. I believe that you were searching. That search will be a long one.'

'What will I discover at the end?' Packo asked.

'You'll find yourself.'

'But I don't understand that,' Packo objected. 'I mean, how can I find myself?'

'You'll find yourself by losing yourself.' Marsha spoke softly, fervently. Packo suspected that a simple truth had been set before him. So simple he couldn't understand any of it.

'You find yourself on the fringe, don't you, Packo. You are not content with the hare's way of life. You're different.'

'Different! My mother used to tell me that. I don't want to be different. I just want to be ordinary, like everyone else.'

'What you really want,' Marsha told him, 'is not to be lonely. Once you learn to lose yourself, you'll never be lonely again. You may be alone, but you'll never be lonely.'

'What's the difference?' Packo asked.

'The difference is in the mind, lose yourself and you'll gain that state of mind.'

'Are you lost?' Packo enquired wickedly.

Marsha laughed, his eyes rolled and his whiskers twitched. 'My young friend, I've been lost for a very long time, and believe me, it's beautiful. Now, listen, enough of this talk. We're well rested, shall we move on?'

'To your form?'

'Yes,' Marsha answered. 'You remember what I told you about running.'

Packo nodded.

Marsha turned and gingerly worked his way clear of the hedge. The temperature had risen and it was snowing again, a soft, lazy fall.

Packo heeded Marsha's earlier advice. He kept his head low, his breathing shallow. Amazingly he found that even after they had been travelling at speed for some time, he was not gulping for air. Marsha occasionally glanced back and smiled when he saw his companion tucked in behind him.

They were traversing a vast, treeless plain, two small creatures insignificant in the immensity around them. Marsha would not have dared use this route had the weather not closed in again. Had it been a clear night they would have been easy prey for the great white owls who patrolled the skies. Now they were virtually invisible.

Packko did not attempt to think too much as he kept pace. He felt a warm glow, felt the need now to live. He was at a threshold. His anger had subsided. Destiny had sent Marsha. He wished nothing more than to learn, and hope that in his learning he might find meaning. He almost bumped into Marsha when they did eventually stop.

'We're here,' Marsha announced.

Packo looked around. They were at the base of a very ancient oak tree, a snow drift heaped against the massive trunk. Packo's puzzled expression made it obvious to Marsha that he was not sure where exactly he was supposed to be.

'Follow me,' Marsha advised.

He led the way around the trunk. The ground fell away and formed a hollow. The snow was not as deep on the leeward side and Marsha scooped some of it away before snapping his teeth shut on a branch which had become visible. He tugged hard and as the branch came free a narrow tunnel opened in front of them. Marsha thrust himself in and disappeared in a swirl of snow. Packo followed. A few seconds later he broke into a cavern, the roof of which was supported by the gnarled roots of the tree. Dry leaves and grass covered the floor which extended for some six or seven lengths. The width, at the centre, was almost four lengths.

Suddenly, Packo felt dizzy and nauseous. His legs buckled and he flopped to the ground, blackness engulfing him. He was alone, shivering in a long, dark tunnel. He was lost, surrounded by emptiness. He was outside, the land barren, desolate. 'You'll find yourself by losing yourself.' The words burned into his semi-consciousness, confusing and baffling him.

▲▼▲

'You slept much better last night.' The voice was gentle, caring.

Packo came to: 'Oh, Marsha.'

'You've been ill, very ill for a long time, almost six weeks, and I blame myself. I failed to appreciate how weak you were.'

'I can remember you finding me, remember your story. It's all very vivid to me. I followed you here, and then . . .'

Marsha smiled, 'How would you like a pleasant surprise?' He gave Packo no opportunity to answer. 'Follow me.'

Packo did as he was bid, blinking back the tears as his eyes tried to accommodate to the unaccustomed daylight. 'Where has it all gone?' he asked incredulously, 'where's all the snow?'

'Spring has arrived at last,' Marsha announced, 'new life.'

'I had thought that I'd never see green fields again,' Packo marvelled. 'Marsha, I owe you my life, thank you.'

A bond was forged between them. Marsha accepted Packo, humbly, as a friend. He readily agreed to share his knowledge believing that availability is the very essence of losing oneself. That spring, as the buds began to burst forth and the grasses once more woke from their dormancy, the lessons began. Winter survival was first on the agenda.

'Shelter from the elements,' Marsha advised. 'Sometimes it is better not to attempt to best them. In a winter like the one we've just experienced the most pertinent thing to remember is that you need somewhere warm in order to survive. You need food too, but you must find shelter. Always avoid the east wind, it brings snow and bitter cold. The north wind can also be savage. The ideal spot for a makeshift form is in their lee. As for food, if you have not thought to store any, find a stream. Dig away the snow along the bank, you'll find withered grass there. Hazel trees have nuts scattered beneath them; oaks, acorns; walnuts, well, walnuts! I'll show you how to recognise these trees, even in winter. Beware of any brightly coloured berries, they can be killers. If the birds won't touch them, leave well alone.'

Each day they roamed the countryside and Packo learned its secrets. His strength gradually built up and he blossomed into adulthood, strong, assured, and, most important of all, happy. Marsha decided that it was time to find out just how strong and confident he was.

'Fancy a bit of a swim?' Marsha asked Packo one day.

Packo's reply was a nervous laugh.

'No need to worry, you already know how really. It's simply a matter of proving it to yourself. Follow me.'

Marsha led the way, running swiftly, head low, breathing in shallow gasps. Packo kept pace on his right shoulder.

'How quickly can you run?' Marsha shouted across.

'I've never really tried to find out,' Packo answered.

'Let's try,' Marsha grinned.

Marsha's sudden explosion surprised Packo. He found himself trailing by six or seven paces. He studied Marsha's hind legs, noticed them driving hard, pushing, fast and furious, using every muscle, extracting every ounce of energy. They had run quickly before, but compared to the pace Marsha now set, that had been no more than brisk. With all the power he could muster Packo tried to close the gap which yawned between them. He could only maintain it as it was.

They ran for some minutes, and not once did Marsha slacken. There was an exhilaration in their running, in their pursuit of speed and excellence. Their softly textured hair was pressed firmly against their bodies by the draught. Their long ears were laid back, offering no resistance to the free-flowing wind created by their speed. Their hind legs pumped power easily, their front paws hardly seemed to touch the ground as they streaked along. They were two graceful creatures fashioned to race the wind, to flash like lightning across the countryside.

Then, quite without warning, Packo began to feel pain. His heart began to pound, its momentum building to a wild thumping in his chest. His breathing, so regulated and controlled, became brisker, his need to take air more pronounced. His hind legs, so strong and sure, began to scream for respite: his front paws, so light and steady, began to dread their next contact with the ground. His side ached with a cutting, dissecting pain.

Yet, Marsha charged on, on and on oblivious to Packo's agony. Packo fought through the first barrier, caught his second breath and everything was fine. Before long, however, the anguish returned more acutely than before.

Packo summoned all of his will power for one, final, effort.

He cast his pain aside, shaking it off like moulting summer hair. He was choking, fighting for breath. His eyes were wild. He was running faster than he had ever run in his life, every ounce of energy was channelled into the task. Now his mind was blank, nulled and cauterized by sheer exertion. Pain no longer mattered, only speed was important.

Then, six paces ahead Marsha slowed and drew up. Packo ground to a halt in front of him. He searched frantically for air, his throat was on fire, his heart pounded, his legs tingled, his stomach ached; he felt terrific! Then he noticed Marsha. He could scarcely believe his eyes. Marsha was doubled up, his back arched, his hind legs drawn up nearly touching his short forelegs. He was gasping huge gulps of air.

Gradually Packo recovered. He approached Marsha who was still crouched and breathing hoarsely. He placed a paw on his back. 'You all right?' he asked.

Marsha nodded vigorously. When he did speak his voice was a croak. 'I will be . . . soon.' He continued to gulp air and, as his heartbeat slowed and his need to gulp air subsided, he sat up on his hind legs and stared at Packo who had completely recovered.

'Who taught you to run like that?' Marsha asked,

'I was only trying to keep up with you,' Packo replied.

'Very nearly killed me, you did.' Marsha's eyes danced playfully. 'I have not been run as hard as that in many a long day. Age must be creeping up on me. Every time I rotated my eyes you never showed any sign of distress. I tried to break you — but, oh no! You kept at it. You were going to catch me, you know. Well! I feel great now, how about you?'

'I'm fine. You know, if we really set our minds to it, we could go faster. We need to work on our stamina.'

Marsha twitched his whiskers. 'You're right of course,' he replied, 'The swimming will help us build up our stamina. You haven't forgotten that that's why we came here?'

Packo had, and he wished that Marsha had too. 'Where's the water?' he asked.

'This way.'

Marsha trotted sedately across a short, open tract of land towards a copse of tall, budding beech trees. They arrived abruptly at the foot of a sharp incline. Beneath them a glassy sheen reflected from the lake's surface.

'Wow!' Packo gasped, amazed at the expanse of water.

'Just remember one thing,' Marsha advised, 'swimming is natural. So, once you are in the water, be natural. There's something rather curious which I must tell you: if you begin to sink, don't try to fight, let yourself go, relax, and you'll come to the surface. Understand?'

Packo nodded reluctantly. He was quite unconvinced and wanted none of it. Marsha noticed his reluctance.

'On the count of three, jump. One . . .'

Packo heard no more. Marsha pushed him headlong over the incline. For an instant he was falling through the air. Then his body cut into the water and he felt the cold envelop him. Down he sank, kicking furiously. The more he kicked and struggled, the deeper he sank.

Then he relaxed and suddenly he began to rise. His head broke through the top and he breathed deeply. Automatically he kicked his hind legs and he was propelled forward, streaking the surface. He was swimming, and it was great fun.

'Bravo, bravo,' Marsha shouted from the bank. He leapt into the air, flying high. He smashed into the water beside Packo and disappeared momentarily. He surfaced and breathed deeply.

'Now we dive,' he called. 'Take a deep breath, tuck your head into your chest, and plunge. And don't forget to open your eyes!'

Packo followed Marsha's lead. They dived to the bottom of the lake and swam along its bed. It was murky and grey. And yet, fascinatingly, here was a whole new world. Sticklebacks darted before them and small roach rested motionless amidst the reeds and swaying grasses. They turned upwards and broke through the surface, gulped air, and again dived to the depths.

It was some time before they clambered on to the muddy shoreline more than a hundred paces from their original point of entry. Instinctively they shook themselves, vigorously spraying the ground and each other. Packo fell into a fit of laughter, laughing until his sides ached. He couldn't remember having ever enjoyed himself so much. Marsha also began to laugh without really knowing why. A piercing cry stopped their laughter. The howl was terrifying. It bit through the air, charging the atmosphere like a streak of lightning. Both hares fell silent immediately, sensing tragedy.

'Come,' Marsha whispered. He crept stealthily towards a cluster of young aspen trees which trembled in the breeze. He paused and pricked his ears. He detected a murmuring, and then a groan. He beckoned Packo to follow amongst the still dormant wild raspberry canes. He was near the centre of the thicket when he found what he had been looking for, a shallow form. The sight of the hare he found shocked him to the core.

His coat appeared to have been torn out in huge chunks revealing patches of congealed blood. One ear had been bitten half off, the other was lacerated near the skull and was hanging loosely. The fur immediately above the paw pads was non-existent and, as Marsha crouched to examine the legs, he noticed that the pads themselves were raw. A dried trickle of blood blocked one of the nostrils, one eye was completely closed by a large swelling above it, and the head was spattered with mud.

The dying hare sensed their presence and shuddered in fear. His rib cage poked through the bare skin and his breathing was noisy and laboured. He made an effort to move.

'We're friends,' Marsha assured him, 'friends come to help. Who inflicted these terrible injuries on you?'

'You will help?' the hare asked. His voice was a hoarse whisper grating through an inflamed throat.

'We'll help,' Marsha said urgently, realising that the hare was slipping away.

'The Land of Deep Shadow,' he groaned. With supreme effort he raised his head. His one open eye, inflamed and watery, pleaded with them. 'The Land of Deep Shadow,' he repeated.

His head slumped to the ground. His body lay limp. The words meant nothing to them.

'. . . life is like a series of journeys and sometimes it might appear that we are going nowhere. Try not to be discouraged, for even in our darkest moments a presence is there. Occasionally, when least expected, this presence, like a silent running companion, will make itself known. Listen to the presence then, heed its words . . .'

Prophecy of Tuarug 3 : 14-15

PART TWO: The Journey

Chapter Six

'The land in the far north, where the cold bites and the earth is tunnelled. There our kind are held in slavery. Rancour and hatred fill the air.'

Marsha turned and stared. Packo was sitting bolt upright, his ears pricked, his gaze fixed and faraway. The words were his, spoken as if in a trance.

'My brothers, I appeal to you, come to us, aid us. For too long our enemies have enslaved us in the dark dungeons of despair where our leverets are born into captivity, never to feel the wind on their backs or view the pale moon across the landscape. I beseech you, come now, we await you.'

Packo shuddered, as if he was shaking off some strange, sinister spirit. He crouched, seeking assurance from the ground, needing its firm contact.

Marsha touched his forepaw with his own. 'You all right?' he asked.

Packo's eyes narrowed, his brow was furrowed. 'What happened?'

'What do you think happened?' Marsha probed gently.

'I spoke words but I don't know where they came from. What does all this mean?'

'It means that we have to find the Land of Deep Shadow,' Marsha replied simply.

'The Land of Deep Shadow.' Packo trembled. 'Why does that name evoke such dread in me?'

'Because there, wherever it is, you will find your destiny,' Marsha responded easily.

Packo was dumbfounded.

'Come,' Marsha urged, 'let us cover this poor hare, put him to rest.'

'Please,' Packo said. 'It is something which I must do.' He remembered Dersall's dead body and how he had callously abandoned it. Perhaps he could begin to atone for the manner in which he had treated his sister.

Marsha nodded and left silently. He worked his way out of the thicket and sat pondering the strange events. Packo carefully broke young budding suckers and laid them over the dead hare until the body was completely hidden from view. His task done, he rejoined Marsha.

'Come,' Marsha said, 'let's go back to the oak, eat and catch some sleep. We'll leave at first light.'

By the time they had returned Packo felt tired. His eyes were heavy and he lay down, falling into a dreamless sleep. Marsha nibbled at a few blades of grass. He wasn't hungry, and neither was he ready to sleep. Packo's words and trance-like delivery stuck in his mind. He had heard of similar happenings before but he had never witnessed one at first hand. He now realised that Packo belonged to a very select group called the Seers. He realised too that Packo probably did not appreciate the significance of what had happened. Marsha had appreciated that Packo was different but he had not considered that he might be a Seer. No one could explain the phenomenon. Through the Seers the sufferings of others were transmitted. Through their sometimes harrowing visions the jaws of evil could be glimpsed. The Seer always spoke of the great calamities of his age, he brought to light injustice and misery. One who witnesses a Seer must act on what he hears . . .

Marsha had been chosen to accompany Packo. Nothing would ever be the same again.

Packo awoke as he felt the prolonged prodding in his side.

'It is time,' Marsha said quietly.

The words shook the sleep from him. The Journey was about to begin. Sometimes it is wiser to step into the dark than to remain in the light.

Marsha closed the den, skilfully concealing its entrance. He turned to Packo.

'May the One who ordains all things protect us and be with us.'

Packo was silent for a moment, considering the words. 'We must head north,' he said. 'When we need to know more, we will be told.'

They travelled all day, stopping occasionally to feed. As night fell they found a safe place to sleep. Early next day they continued. Day after day they pressed northwards. Neither complained, nor did either entertain any idea of giving up. Piece by piece all would be revealed; they did not doubt that, even for an instant.

The flat, patchwork fields gave way to low, undulating hills. Towards evening on the second day of travel across the hills they came to a forest planted with Sitka spruce and tall, elegant Douglas fir. The new panorama was welcome; it marked another stage of their journey.

'It shouldn't be difficult to find a cosy spot to rest among that lot,' Marsha said, clearly relishing the change of scenery.

They raced into the darkness of the tightly packed trees. Here no sun warmed the ground which was clear of grass and ferns. The strong, pungent odour of pine pervaded the still atmosphere, and the silence was absolute. Nothing stirred; could it be that nothing lived?

Packo paused. Marsha, sensing that something was wrong, looked on.

'Marsha, Marsha,' Packo whispered urgently.

'What is it?' Marsha asked, finding himself also whispering.

Packo's eyes narrowed. He summoned every sense he possessed to probe the hidden, lurking thing that watched their every move. 'There is great peril here.'

'We could go back and try to skirt around the trees,' Marsha suggested, knowing that he must heed Packo's warning.

'No, no,' Packo was emphatic, 'this is the way, we must continue though it may cost us our lives. This is the way.'

'Well, we could find a safe place to rest for the night,' Marsha suggested.

'No, we must meet this evil, now is the time.'

'Right, let's move it.'

Packo tucked in closely to Marsha's rear. They stole on, nimbly, stealthily, like usurpers in some dark lord's demesne. All around black tree trunks vaulted an invisible sky. The further they progressed, the more oppressive the atmosphere grew, the pine aroma bearing heavily upon them like a massive pall. They were moving ever deeper into the brooding night.

The hairs rising on Packo's neck were the first indication that the siege was about to begin. They came from the darkness above. They moved silently, their flight feathers surfaced and tipped with down. Their eyes glimmered behind razor sharp beaks and their flared talons were poised, ready to sink into their prey. These were the long-eared owls who patrolled the pine forest, never venturing from its confines, aware of every trespasser, ever ready to kill intruders.

'Take cover!' Packo shouted.

Marsha too had become aware of the threat. Immediately he veered away to his right: Packo automatically broke left. This confused the leading owl whose prey had departed from his flight path. He tucked his right wing in slightly and pursued Marsha. Another owl followed while four tracked Packo. The two hares flashed across the forest floor passing under broken boughs. Each knew exactly what to do. They cut out a quarter circle. When Marsha had travelled wide enough, he issued a high-pitched call. He then cut to his left along the invisible diameter. Packo reacted instantly to the message, broke to his right, and started upon a direct collision course with Marsha.

They passed within a whisker of each other and then heard

the confused shrieks of their adversaries, two of whom collided heavily, forcing them earthwards. One broke a wing, the other suffered severely bruised ribs. The remaining four owls soared into the deep darkness above. Marsha again echoed a shrill call, summoning Packo.

They tore forward to the heart of the forest. They found a spot where several thick tree trunks had fallen almost to the ground, their rotting lengths caught by saplings. They rested in the blackness beneath a tangle of exposed roots on top of which a heaving pine balanced precariously.

'You all right?' Marsha asked.

'Fine,' Packo smiled. 'Shall we dig in here, wait until morning?'

'That's what they'll be expecting us to do and as soon as we move they'll be waiting. Even in daylight the shadows will be deep and not much sunlight will penetrate. No great advantage to us. Either way, we are in their territory and our only chance is to keep them guessing by doing what they don't expect. I imagine that they will have gathered their forces by now and will be lying in wait. Let's give them a little while to settle, make them believe that we are going to stay here until morning. They must think that they have the advantage. Then we'll make a break for it. You game?'

'Not their game, I hope!' Packo replied.

Marsha's eyes gleamed. 'Perhaps we'll show them a thing or two.'

They lay acutely aware of the menacing silence. If the owls were gathering they gave no clue.

'Ready?' Marsha whispered at last. Packo stood. 'One piece of advice, Packo. We'll separate often and keep in touch by calling. If you change direction always do so immediately you have passed a tree, not before. That way you'll show less of yourself and make life awkward for them. That's the name of the game. We'll race out together and stay that way until we know that they are on to us. Then . . . well, you know.'

'I know,' Packo assured him, 'don't worry.'

Marsha stood for a moment summoning his strength and determination. He nudged Packo and together they rushed into the darkness. In the eerie silence it seemed their passing had gone unnoticed.

The owls had regrouped. Two were no longer able to participate but the four who remained were confident that they would bring the spoils home. This time they attacked head on, bearing down on the hares from a position they suspected would cause confusion. That it did not was thanks to the ever alert Marsha. He saw their coming, waited until their large round eyes seemed to fill his line of vision, and shouted, 'Split.' The hares instantly changed direction and the owls were left perplexed at their alacrity.

To the owls, however, the hares' escape represented only a stay of execution. A flap of their mighty wings and they soared upwards. They knew instinctively where the boughs of the trees reached out to caress one another and were able to avoid contact with them. They circled nonchalantly, their ultra-sensitive hearing able to detect the most minute sound on the forest floor. The two hares were easily discovered, running a northerly parallel course some forty paces apart. They had separated. Excellent! The owls split, the spoils could be shared.

Packo spotted his assailants stalking him once more. They kept their distance. Here, in the very heart of the forest, there was plenty of cover for a small creature. He realised that they were allowing him to go on, biding their time until he reached a clearing. He knew what to do. If he could conceal himself, disappear from their view, they would have to come looking for him. Perhaps then the advantage might swing marginally in his favour. He ducked under a fallen tree and, instead of emerging from the other side, halted and crept near the base of the uprooted trunk. He waited. Within moments he felt the rush of wind as one owl approached to investigate. Then the other flew overhead. 'Ho-oo-oo,' one called. Had they seen him or was that a question passed from one to the other? Roughly thirty paces ahead he spotted several dead branches, tangled shapes rising from the ground like stakes protecting an ancient fortification. An idea formed in his mind. It involved great risk but if he was to escape he would have to wrest the initiative from the owls. The time had come to fight back.

He streaked from his place of concealment. Immediately the owls came out of the night, their beaks thrust forward. They had remained out of sight for precisely this purpose, to force their prey into one final act of panic. Now they had him.

Packo rotated his eyes and saw their approach. He slowed slightly, wanting to reach the branches at just the right moment. The owls were no more than three paces away when he jumped into the middle of the dead wood. As he landed a branch was catapulted into the air striking the leading owl across the span of his left wing, fracturing bones. Packo kicked hard with his hind legs and sent a piece of timber flying. It struck the second owl in the chest, ruffling his plumage. He dropped to the ground, stunned. Packo leapt towards him with lightning speed and plunged a forepaw punch between his eyes. The creature lay still. The other owl was flapping his good wing furiously while the damaged one lay bedraggled by his side, bent and broken. Now to find Marsha.

He hurried on continuing his northerly course. He had travelled some minutes before he recognised a familiar call. He raced over and found Marsha sitting up, peering into the blackness.

'What kept you, Packo?' he asked.

Packo scanned the air. 'Where are they?'

'Indisposed. And yours?'

'Indisposed.' They smiled at each other.

'Let's find a safe place,' Marsha suggested, 'and then you can tell me all about it.'

Fewer trees seemed to have fallen in this area but Marsha, always able to sniff out a safe resting place, found a shallow depression and dragged the nearest piece of debris he could find, a branch still smelling pungently of pine, to cover it. They crawled underneath, snug and safe from prying eyes. Packo told his story simply, realising he had been lucky.

'You made your own luck, Packo,' Marsha commented.

'So, come on,' Packo urged, 'what happened to your two pursuers?'

'Well, I must admit,' Marsha began, 'that fortune favoured me. I was concentrating on making them work, annoying them, trying to ensure that the hunt was as difficult as possible. I would allow them a sight of me, then I would disappear. They passed very close several times and they were becoming agitated. However, I had no real plan to throw them. Then, accidentally, I snagged one of my hind legs on something, a broken branch I suspect. As I ran into a clearing I was unaware that I was leaving a trail of blood. I disappeared from view again. The owls glided past, very close. They had become very excited. It was then that I realised that I was bleeding, that they had caught the scent or spotted the trail. Their natural instincts took over and they began to vie for first place. Until then I had been a prize to be shared. Now I became an object of their blood lust. Whoever caught me would demand that he alone savour the kill.

'I lived more dangerously still. I attempted to toy with them, avoiding their grasp by the merest fraction. Their frenzy mounted but my injury was not serious and I ran to a clearing between the trees. I crouched there, feeling naked. I saw them approach, flashing out of the darkness, electrified by the sight of me lying there so still, finally run to ground. They were very close when I feinted, first to the left near to one, then to the right, near the other. I was trying to tease them, and it worked. I was within the grasp of one and the other owl knocked him away. Well, a real fracas broke out. Scratching bits out of each other they were, ripped plumage and blood everywhere. I left them to it and went in search of you.'

Packo was silent for a moment. 'Marsha,' he said, 'someone, somewhere, is watching over us,'

'I know,' Marsha acknowledged, 'otherwise, we could never have survived this evening.'

'But who, and why?'

'I've really no idea, Packo, I've said to you before that I believe nothing ever happens by chance, by so-called coincidence. There is a purpose, and that purpose is with us now. All we can do is hope to gain understanding by continuing our search.'

They settled down, weary after the day's trek and the evening's drama. When they awoke the heavy night darkness of the forest had lifted. They decided to drive on, to find the land where the trees gave way.

Finally, after a long day's journey, they emerged into the red light of a setting sun. The tree line behind them was thick and ran in either direction to distant horizons. Marsha halted abruptly and turned back to face the trees just behind them. He cocked his ears, sniffed and studied the forest. He had sensed something. Packo remained silent.

Directly in front of them, perhaps five or six paces away at the very edge of the forest, a hare hopped into their line of vision. He was old and wizened, a buck whose bright eyes belied his age.

'Marsha, Packo, I greet you.' The voice was strong, sure, mesmerising. 'You have passed through the dark woods successfully. Well done! Continue your northerly course. Be vigilant, you will meet friend and foe along your way. When you reach the great sea follow the shoreline until you reach the Chaos Chasm. There your courage will be tested.'

Marsha and Packo glanced at one another, both unsure of what to make of this apparition. When they looked back the old hare had disappeared. Marsha bounded forward, sniffing and gazing in every direction.

Packo sat still, pondering the old hare's words. He knew that Marsha's search would be fruitless.

Chapter Seven

The sun was beginning to flood the western horizon, spilling blood across the darkening sky. Marsha and Packo had travelled for a full day following the strange encounter with the old hare. They were well pleased to be out in the open again, to see the clear sky overhead, to feel the breeze against their pelts and smell the freshness of spring producing life from the earth.

They had crossed a field sown with winter wheat. The green shoots were sprouting from the earth, growing stronger as the warm weather returned. Marsha was scanning the area in search of a suitable form in which to spend the night. They passed through a hawthorn hedge. They were about to move forward when they were confronted by four hares who jumped from the hedge and blocked their way.

The leader of the group was an extremely large buck, overfed and slovenly. His three companions, also bucks, were much smaller and stood behind him arrogantly, safe in his presence.

'What have we here then?' the big buck asked. He answered himself, 'A pair of hares, strangers, trespassing on our turf. We don't like trespassers, do we lads?'

He was answered by an assortment of grunts and nods as if the other three were merely puppets with lolling heads.

'That's right, lads,' he continued. 'We don't like strangers. So, you two, where do you think you're going?'

'We're just passing through, making our way to the field over there to find a form for the night.' Marsha's voice was steady, his stare was directed straight into the eyes of the large hare.

'Just passing through,' the large hare said, 'minding your own business, I suppose?'

'Correct,' Marsha confirmed.

'Well, it's been quiet around here recently, hasn't it lads?'

Assorted grunts.

'We could do with a bit of fun, couldn't we lads?'

Lolling heads.

'How about you fight for the right to pass through our turf?'

Marsha remained composed. He knew that he could take this overweight bully if he had to. He was thinking of Packo. How would he react if the other three turned nasty?

Unknown to Marsha, Packo was calm and unafraid and he had an idea.

'Hey!' Packo shouted as he pushed forward, prodding Marsha with a forepaw. 'Why should you have all the fun? I'll fight him.'

Marsha was caught off guard and then he recognised the glint in Packo's eye. He sprang into action.

'You can't take him, look at him.'

Packo looked.

'Hmmm. He's a bag of wind, all wind. He's obese.'

Marsha turned to the large hare. 'You probably don't understand that. He says you're a fat slob.'

'Why, the little . . .'

Marsha didn't allow the fat slob to finish. 'I'll sort him out, you leave him to me.' Back to Packo, 'Always fancying yourself, that's your trouble. Well, I intend to knock the lard out of you.'

Marsha slapped Packo across the snout. Packo reacted dramatically.

'Oh yeah,' he screamed vehemently. 'I've had enough of your mouth. First you, then Fatso.'

Marsha smiled at Fatso. 'I'm so sorry,' he apologised, 'I'll be with you in a moment.'

They met head on, exchanging blows which carried no weight. The large hare looked on, mesmerised. Somehow, he had lost control. Now Marsha had his forepaws round Packo's neck. 'Roll with me,' he whispered, 'one side each.' They fell to the ground scuffling, rolling over and over until they were very near the large hare.

'Now,' Marsha shouted.

With their powerful hind legs each delivered a perfectly aimed kick on either side of the large hare's rib cage. He howled. Marsha immediately aimed a second blow to his head, knocking him senseless. Fatso was out for the count.

Packo had already caught one of the puppets with a punch to the snout, drawing blood. Marsha rushed to help but there was no need. Without a leader they shot off wildly.

'You never cease to amaze me,' Marsha told Packo, 'How did you come to think of that scam?'

'I remembered something you once said to me about doing the unexpected. Let's go and find that form and rest a while.'

They left the large hare to his dreams. He would wake later a little sore for his trouble-making and, hopefully, a little wiser. They quickly found some thick grass and settled down. The night air was cool, fresh and welcoming.

Packo did not know how long he had slept. He felt an insistent prodding in his flank which, at first, he instinctively tried to move away from. To no avail. It moved with him.

'Packo, Packo, wake up!'

He opened his eyes. It was still dark.

'Packo,' Marsha murmured, 'be alert, there's trouble out there.'

Packo focused his mind and stared out into the darkness. For several moments nothing happened. Then, some twenty paces ahead, he spotted a movement. He thought he noticed, out of the corner of his eye, another off to his left. He caught the merest glimpse of a flitting dark shape. Something out there was stalking them.

'They probably think that we're asleep,' Marsha told him, his voice barely audible. 'Let's keep whoever it is thinking that way. Be ready to move.'

They waited, ears pricked against the slightest noise or movement. Marsha had an all round view. He knew that there were five creatures in front and three to the rear. Extraordinary really! If he had wished to stalk someone his main forces would have been behind with a token number in front to turn the prey. He concluded that whoever was out there didn't have too much experience. If that was the case it followed that Packo and himself were not being hunted for food. Predators would be more cunning. Who was out there, and why?

Then the silence was broken.

'You are surrounded, there is no escape.' The voice wavered, its unsteadiness betraying the speaker's lack of confidence.

'We'll go along with it,' Marsha whispered to Packo, 'stay put.'

'All right,' Marsha answered, 'I'm coming out.' He pressed out of the form. A thin, ragged-looking hare came forward to confront him. He was immediately joined by four younger hares, their darting eyes betraying their nervousness. Marsha moved away from Packo's place of concealment. He was playing a hunch that these hares did not realise that there were two of them. The three hares from the rear joined their companions.

'Is there a problem?' Marsha asked frankly.

'Well . . .' The leader glanced at his fellows. 'I . . . I think we may have been in error.'

The explanation suddenly dawned on Marsha. 'Perhaps,' he suggested, 'you thought I was that fat slob who has been terrorising this area?'

Their surprise was evident on their faces.

'Well, not exactly,' the ragged hare replied. 'We were hoping that you might be one of his companions, one of our own whom we wish to persuade to desert the large hare. Obviously you are not.'

Marsha turned briefly. 'Packo,' he called, 'it's all right, we're among friends.' As he expected, Packo's appearance produced more startled faces.

'We're not very good at this sort of thing,' the ragged hare said, 'we thought you were alone. I'm sorry if we frightened you.'

Marsha felt the genuineness in the hare's voice, the honest simplicity of decent creatures.

Packo stepped forward. 'I'm Packo,' he announced, 'you've met Marsha. Perhaps if you told us what's going on we may be able to help.'

The ragged hare smiled for the first time. 'I'd like to do that, and we should be very grateful for any advice. My name is Litrel and I am the elder of the colony of hares which has lived in these parts for generations. For as long as I can remember we have been happy here. No one ever bothered us and we never experienced trouble. That is part of our predicament. You see, we never fight. We discuss our differences in our Hares' Parliament, a gathering of everyone in our community, bucks, does, and leverets. The Parliament decides issues and we all abide by the majority decision. None of us has known anything but peace. That changed recently when the large hare arrived in our midst.

'We greeted him cordially, respecting his right to the land which is not ours to possess, only to share. He accepted our friendship and was thus able to infiltrate our group. He terrorised some of our younger bucks into joining him and he began to bully and dictate his evil ways. As elder of our community I admonished him publicly. He set about me, tearing my fur out, beating me. He might easily have killed me but he wanted an example for the rest. He warned that any who opposed him could expect to experience even worse. We live in his shadow. He controls us by threat and innuendo. You must understand that we do not condone violence, nor do we practise it. It is alien to all that we hold sacred.

'A few nights ago a shocking event occurred. A very young doe was attacked and left for dead. She survived the horror and was able to describe her assailant, the large hare. Our plan has been to endeavour to isolate his young followers, to attempt to speak reason to them. Perhaps then the large hare might leave us alone. We thought you were one of his followers; we wished only to speak with you.'

'You say a young doe was attacked?' Marsha asked. 'What would be the penalty for such a crime?'

'It has never happened before,' Litrel assured him, 'but we have agreed that the punishment should be exile. The problem is we cannot enforce the punishment. We simply do not know how to fight.'

'But you do believe in fair play, in justice?' Marsha asked.

'Of course, of course,' Litrel replied emphatically, almost offended that any other thought might pass through Marsha's mind.

'Therefore,' Marsha said, 'the large hare should face his accuser, have an opportunity to answer the charge?'

'In normal circumstances one accused would stand before the Parliament, certainly.'

'And how quickly can you convene your Parliament?'

'Oh, within a very short time. But why?'

'Because we will deliver the large hare to you very shortly. Be ready, here. Come on Packo, let's go fetch Fatso.'

The night was still dark and Marsha was gambling that the large hare had found a form in which to rest, lick his wounds, and nurse his pride. They were quickly back at the spot where they had met him. The grass on which he had lain was pressed down, but he was gone. Marsha examined the ground minutely and beckoned Packo to follow as he picked up the trail. It ran alongside the hedge for a mere ten paces and then he detected where the grass had been flattened and the hawthorn hedge entered. Silently he instructed Packo to take up a position on his right, then he moved forward gingerly.

The breathing was laboured and painful. It drew Marsha to a spot immediately in front of him. He peered in and caught sight of the large hare, his obese body filling the gap into which he had crawled. He had obviously chosen his haven quickly. In the event of an emergency the entrance was his only exit. That was a mistake.

Marsha stole forward and delivered a swift, telling blow into the large hare's rib cage, picking the spot that had been injured earlier. The large hare howled and woke with a start, grimacing with pain, fear flowing from his eyes.

'We have business to attend to,' Marsha told him authoritatively. 'Come with us quietly, or we'll knock you senseless and drag you.'

The large hare was bemused.

'Seems you've been causing friends of ours a little bother,' Marsha said menacingly. 'Time to answer for your crimes.'

The large hare raised himself slowly, painfully. Then he sprang out of his form, attempting to smother Marsha with his obese body. Marsha, however, was ready. He backed away speedily, moved to his left, and allowed the large hare to land, painfully, beside the hedge. Marsha and Packo moved in immediately, delivering savage hind leg kicks to the large hare's flanks. Marsha dashed around and aimed a heavy slap across the large hare's snout.

'You can come quietly,' Marsha warned, 'or we can finish it here. Your choice.'

The large hare raised his spinning head. Marsha and Packo filled his vision. The pain in his side screamed. Yes, he preferred a quiet passage.

Packo led the way back while Marsha kept a watchful eye on their captive. There was little for him to be concerned about. The large hare was labouring, his body ached, he was sore and full of shocks. Packo had not spoken during the encounter. A recurring thought plagued him. Some purpose was being served here, something which would help them in their quest for the Land of Deep Shadow.

Their return to Litrel seemed to take forever. The large hare really was hurting. He groaned occasionally and tended to lean to his right in an attempt to alleviate his pain. He was a wretched sight, a great grotesque heap of dripping flesh.

They came at last to where the hares had gathered, thirty or so, sitting in a circle. Marsha marched into the centre and peered into the intent, nervous faces surrounding him. Packo pushed his snout under Fatso, bundling him forward. He moaned and staggered and slumped to the ground. Litrel stepped to the centre.

'You must answer for your crimes before the Parliament,' he announced, his eyes resting on the sorry hare in front of him.

The large hare gazed at him, his face as limp as his gait.

'Who accuses this hare?' Litrel asked.

The silence was absolute. Litrel allowed it to hang. Suddenly there was a shuffle from the circle's perimeter. A young, fragile doe stepped forward. She was unsure of her footing and in obvious distress. Her large brown eyes were sunk deep into their sockets and her ripped fur revealed long scratches along her flanks. She struggled gamely to the centre and faced the large hare.

'I accuse you,' she said, her voice weak but firm. 'You attacked me two evenings ago, you beat me.'

The large hare's eyes narrowed slightly.

Suddenly, and to everyone's amazement, the doe swung one of her forepaws, slapping the large hare across his face. Blood began to pour from his snout and he hung his head in shame and great terror. The cry went up from the gathered hares, 'Kill, Kill.'

The large hare cowered.

The chant rose higher and higher, more determined and frenzied and vengeful. Litrel was astonished. His peace-loving family had become blood-thirsty brutes. He stood on his hind legs and emitted a long, chilling screech which pierced the ears of all present. They fell silent. Litrel turned slowly, burning his eyes into theirs. Then he spoke.

'A terrible crime has been committed by the hare we have before us. Do we have the right to commit a more terrible crime still?' He paused and his burning eyes again examined those of his listeners. 'The punishment due here has been decided, exile with a warning.' Litrel now centred his attention on the large hare.

'If you ever come here again, you will forfeit your life. Do you understand?'

The large hare maintained his cowering position.

Litrel approached him and, with a strength he did not ordinarily possess, lifted the large hare's head with one of his fore-paws. 'Do you understand?' he insisted.

'Yes.' The reply was little more than a hoarse whisper.

'Now,' Litrel commanded him, 'Go.'

The large hare moved, ponderously, from his squat position. As he neared the circle's circumference two hares stood back to enable him to pass. He shuffled away, eventually disappearing into the undergrowth at the far edge of the field.

Packo watched his departure, knowing that they would meet again.

Chapter Eight

The business of the Parliament over, the hares hopped off in various directions to seek food and murmur among themselves.

Litrel turned to Marsha and Packo. 'That confrontation brought out a side in us I didn't think existed. They might have killed him.'

'Violence leads to violence,' Marsha said. 'Perhaps if ever a similar situation arises again you'll be better able to nip it in the bud by being a little more forceful as a group.'

'Perhaps,' Litrel conceded. 'We owe you a debt of gratitude. Thank you.'

'You're welcome. Now we should rest, then be on our way.'

'Wait.' It was Packo. He was staring hard into the distance, that faraway gaze filling his eyes.

'What is it?' Marsha asked, aware that the Seer's powers were coming through.

'Someone near might be able to advise us, an old hare who lives alone. 'I feel his presence, very close.'

'I know an old hare who lives alone,' Litrel said. 'Perhaps he is the one of whom you speak.'

'Please, could you direct us to him?' Packo asked.

'I will take you to him. He lives half a day's journey from here, directly north across the mountains.'

'Directly north,' the words resounded in Marsha's mind mingling with those of the wizened old hare, 'Continue to follow your northerly course.'

'We'll set off at first light,' Litrel said. 'Come, I'll show you a safe place to catch a few hours sleep.'

'Good idea,' Packo agreed. Marsha nodded.

Litrel led them across the field where perennial grasses bordered a moonbeam hedge. There they settled to await the dawn. Packo was asleep within moments. Marsha lay quietly, wondering, not for the first time, where their travels might be taking them. He drowsed but was alert when Litrel approached just as the first streaks of grey shot over the eastern horizon.

'Time to go,' Litrel told him.

'I'll wake Packo.'

'No need, I'm ready.'

'Come then,' Litrel bade them, 'and I shall be able to return by nightfall.'

He set a sensible pace, one which could be maintained for a long time in comfort and left plenty in reserve should they need to use their formidable turn of speed. As the morning passed, the countryside became more rugged and mountainous. The grass became coarser and random boulders fractured the ground. They began to climb, their legs feeling the strain. Litrel kept his head down in the classic hare's way. His powerful hind legs pushed him on and up until at last the summit was achieved. They had climbed to a surprising height and the view was panoramic. Valleys and hills spread before them and to their right. To their left, silver glimmered in the far distance. Behind them, the dark woods formed a small blot.

'The great sea,' Litrel informed Packo who was gazing at the dappled light away to his left.

Marsha was looking back and, for a split second, thought that he saw a shape move at the bottom of the mountain. He peered hard and long but nothing stirred. His eyes had obviously deceived him, or had they?

'Now we must follow this ridge,' Litrel explained. He loped off once more.

They had changed direction and the great sea became their fixed point of reference.

The ground was fairly level and stony. At times they plunged dramatically before beginning another ascent. Finally Litrel paused. 'Now we must leave the ridge,' he said, 'the old hare lives directly beneath us. Take care not to travel too quickly, lest the steep slope carry you away.'

Gingerly he stepped to his right and by means of awkward sideways movements began the descent. Marsha and Packo imitated him and discovered that it prevented them from careering wildly down the slope. They reached the valley floor quickly. Litrel knew the spot he was seeking and, as soon as the ground levelled, he halted.

'We're here,' he announced.

Marsha and Packo did not understand. The grass was short and offered no place of concealment. Boulders strewn around the ground stood as sentinels guarding the approaches to the verdant valley.

Litrel was aware of their puzzlement. 'I'll show you,' he said, smiling. He hopped to the nearest boulder, sniffed around, and then disappeared from view.

Marsha followed him to the spot and examined the ground. At first he missed the opening. Moss had been cleverly cultivated on a small rock placed to one side. It camouflaged the entrance. He poked his head inside and saw Litrel crouching in a passage, waiting.

'If you didn't know where it was you'd probably miss it,' Litrel observed.

'Amazing,' Marsha replied in admiration.

He stepped in, closely followed by Packo.

Litrel led them down the passageway until they came out into a cavern. A furry shape at the far end threw up its head as they entered.

'Litrel,' an old, kindly voice echoed, 'good to see you, my friend.'

As Marsha and Packo came into view the old hare's eyes opened wide. 'You've brought me visitors, excellent, excellent.'

'Horeb,' Litrel greeted him, 'it's good to see you too. My

friends, Marsha and Packo, wish to consult with you.'

'I'm honoured,' Horeb replied. 'Please, come forward. Let me offer you food and drink.'

'Not for me,' Litrel said. 'Don't think me rude but I cannot stay. We have had a problem recently. Marsha and Packo helped to resolve it. I feel I should be back by nightfall. Marsha and Packo will explain what happened. I will return, as usual, four nights after the new moon. We shall talk then.'

'I shall look forward to that. Take care, my friend.'

Litrel turned to Marsha and Packo. 'Thank you for your assistance, I hope you find what you are seeking.'

He smiled and was gone.

'Any friend of Litrel is a friend of mine,' Horeb told them. 'Please step forward that I might see you. My eyesight is diminishing as age creeps upon me.'

Marsha moved towards him. 'I'm Marsha, and this is Packo.' He turned, expecting to see Packo immediately behind him. He was not there. He was standing rigid by the exit.

Horeb knew that something was wrong. He hopped nearer to Packo sensing a presence. 'We have here a Seer,' he whispered. 'Tell us,' he commanded, 'what do you see?'

'I see persecution and slavery. I see torture, pain, death. I see degradation and hopelessness. And I hear them calling, "Come, come." I shudder and ask, "Me?" They reply, "Come, come." "But where are you?" I ask them. "In the Land of Deep Shadow, there you will find us."'

Horeb stared. 'Land of Deep Shadow!' He had not heard that expression for many moons.

'There is something you can tell us,' Packo said to Horeb, 'some ancient wisdom you have been waiting to impart. Please, tell us.'

Packo shivered, the pupils of his eyes dilated, and he pressed his body to the ground. Horeb remained still, respecting the presence of the Seer, waiting for normality to return. Packo took several deep breaths, shook his head, and gazed intently at the old hare.

'We are here for a purpose, can you help us?' He wanted so much to understand.

'What I can tell you is but a piece of the whole, and only a small piece at that.'

They sat and Horeb began.

'I lead a solitary life here. It is my own choosing. I haven't always lived alone. I spent most of my younger days as a wandering buck. I used to travel, to meet with those whose gathered wisdom was so much greater than mine. I learned from them the secrets of the Ancients, that esoteric knowlege passed down from one generation to the next. Passed down, and yet always elusive.

'I learned that the "Land of Deep Shadow" refers to a semi-mythical land of cold beauty. No one I met had ever been there and many doubted its existence. Some said that its location is a secret still hidden. Perhaps you have been called to unveil that secret. Terrible crimes are said to be committed there, crimes against our own kind. It is a cold place, snow covering the land for many months. It is also a place of great beauty and soft, brief summers.

'That is almost the sum total of my knowledge — not much is it? The land is magnificent, yet full of death. It has remained mythical because no one ever sought it. There is one more thing. The Ancients foretold that one day a hare would receive the call to turn towards the "Land of Deep Shadow". They said that he would face great danger, but through it all, if he persevered, he would meet his destiny.'

Packo was bemused. Surely he couldn't be the one of whom the Ancients had spoken? His mother's words echoed in his mind, 'You have a calling and a destiny; go, find your destiny . . .' But what was this special destiny?

'Do you know where this land lies?' Marsha asked.

'No,' Horeb replied, 'I have never heard anyone speak of its location.'

'We were told to travel north, to reach the great sea and follow its shoreline until we reached the Chaos Chasm.'

Horeb frowned. 'May I ask who gave you this information?'

'A hare who appeared from nowhere, and disappeared just as quickly.'

'A Purveyor!' Horeb looked amazed. 'You saw a Purveyor?'

'I don't know,' Marsha shrugged, 'what's a Purveyor?'

'One who guides the chosen. He appears in order to issue instructions and to offer advice. You are privileged to have seen him.'

Horeb remained silent for a moment, ruminating on his next statement. 'I must warn you, you are undertaking a perilous journey. When you leave here travel directly west; a day will take you to the great sea. Beware the sand dunes, the lands that slink towards the vast waters. They are dangerous and fraught with difficulties. Strangers are not welcome there.'

'Can you be more specific?' Marsha asked.

'Heed my words,' Horeb replied, 'the sand dunes are an evil place.'

'And the Chaos Chasm?' Marsha asked, 'what is that?'

'I have no knowledge of it.'

Silence descended.

It was Packo who eventually stirred. He stood on his hind legs and stretched. 'You know, I'm quite hungry now.'

'A Seer with a practical turn of mind,' Horeb grinned, 'that can't be bad. Come, I'll show you some tender young shoots of grass. They will replenish you.'

He led them from the underground cavern. Horeb was surprised to see that the sun was sinking fast in the western sky. The floor of the valley was a short distance and there they found a plentiful supply of the new season's greenery. They ate leisurely, using the time to relax and forget the journey they had embarked upon so many days previously.

Then they sat and chewed and watched the cloud-flecked sky gradually darken. Marsha experienced a strange peace. Here was a place where one could appreciate being alone. The majestic mountains towered behind them, their summits seeming to touch the very heavens. He felt a great sense of achievement in having ascended one of them further to the east and traversed the ridge almost directly to the point above where they were now relaxing. He followed the course they had taken, reliving the journey, sorry now that he had not taken more time to appreciate the vista their lofty perch had afforded them.

Then he saw it! A sudden movement away to his left, high up on the ridge. He blinked, staring hard. It had vanished. He had cast his earlier sighting from his mind. Now he was sure that he was not imagining things. Was someone up there watching them?

'You must stay the night of course.' Horeb's words broke into his thoughts. 'You'll be better prepared to begin your journey to the great sea.'

'That's very kind of you,' Marsha replied, 'I think that would be best.'

They trooped back to the cavern and settled down. Horeb regaled them with stories, songs, and verses collected during his journeys. No more was mentioned of their intended quest to seek that strange and mythical Land of Deep Shadow. The movements he had observed continually surfaced in Marsha's mind. He was convinced that someone out there was watching them. Another mystery.

Chapter Nine

A fresh, westerly wind greeted them the following morning. Horeb sniffed and allowed it to bite at his twitching snout. 'Rain,' he muttered, 'you can be sure of it. Not for a while yet though, give it a day or two and that wind will bring rain. Still it makes life easy for you, as regards your route, I mean. Just head straight into that wind. You'll arrive at the great sea before nightfall. That wind will still be blowing, building up for the fury that's to come.'

Although his words were addressed to both Marsha and Packo he spoke, as is the wont of those who live much of their lives alone, more to himself than to them. 'Marsha, Packo, you have far to go. Be careful,' he admonished, 'the road ahead is not an easy one. Beware the sand dunes, they hold great terror. Keep to the shore whenever you can. Maybe you will come at last to the Land of Deep Shadow, I don't know. Remember, it is always more important to try than to achieve. Don't be down-hearted. I wish you well.'

They thanked him and then, heads down against the brisk breeze, they set off. They maintained their easy, steady pace. Whatever thoughts passed through their minds were not shared. Silence became the way as their powerful hind legs propelled them forward. Marsha was a seasoned traveller, and although he adopted a relaxed gait, he was ever aware of his surroundings. A hare moving across open territory can never afford to relax. His massive powers of acceleration are always kept in store in the event of an emerging danger. That is what the burst of speed is for. The young, inexperienced hare bolts here and there. The older hare keeps a reserve, his lightning turn often enabling him to escape from his enemy. Having something in reserve is more important than an early arrival.

On this particular day no external dangers presented themselves. They followed the line of the mountains which towered above them away to their left. Eventually these began to fall and peter out and, still some distance off, they got their first good sight of the great sea. What a magnificent sight it was! The waters sparkled and danced like a bed of gleaming diamonds. They were eager to reach it.

The terrain became soft underfoot, low hills clad with patchy marram grass.

'These must be the sand dunes Horeb mentioned,' Marsha said.

'And he warned us to be wary of them,' Packo answered, looking around, half expecting to see something threatening.

'Indeed,' Marsha nodded, beginning to feel ill at ease as he remembered. 'Let's heed that warning and make for the sea.'

He made to run up the next hillock but encountered loose sand and slid back down.

'Perhaps we should make haste slowly,' Packo suggested.

They pressed on. The journey over the shifting sands was tiring and the freshening breeze blew fine grains of sand into their eyes causing them to smart and water. They quickly forgot their discomfort when the ocean finally spread before them, a limitless, twinkling sheet of water stretching into infinity.

'Come on,' Marsha shouted, 'let's get in there.'

They raced to the sea and splashed into it. Packo dipped his head and drank deeply. His eyes widened in horror and his throat contracted forcing the sticky saltiness back out.

'Don't try drinking it,' he shouted to Marsha.

Too late! His experience was every bit as sickly as Packo's. He forced a smile. 'So, we've learned not to drink it, but isn't it terrific.' He turned quickly and kicked his hind legs, showering

Packo with a cascading rainbow. Packo laughed and fought back, spraying water at Marsha. Then they raced and jumped the waves. They roared with laughter and shrieked with delight. Here was a treasure of fun they had never dreamed of. They were absorbed by the magic and mystery of the sea. Time did not matter any more. All thoughts of the future were washed away, worries about the Land of Deep Shadow erased from their minds. They simply enjoyed the present moment and hardly noticed the sinking sun signifying the end of another day.

Finally, they crawled to the water's edge and rested just beyond the waves' reach. The wind had strengthened and it ruffled their pelts as they sat gazing at the immensity before them.

'Hungry?' Marsha asked.

'Tired,' Packo replied wearily.

'We'll find shelter behind the first sand dune. It should be snug there and safe so near to the sea.'

The sea's saltiness stung their snouts as they scooped out the loose sand to form a hollow. They lay down to rest. Sleep came easily and dreams were distant. They had travelled long and played hard.

▲▼▲

The morning dawned grey and sombre. The wind was fresher yet, the tide out, and the sea, far away, choppy and refractory. The two hares nibbled absent-mindedly at the meagre supply of marram grass that had gained some purchase on the leeward side of the sand dunes. They did not speak. The exhilaration of the previous evening left them sober and quiet. Marsha glanced at Packo. It was time to move, time to continue their trek.

They set off, moving away from the sand dunes and finding firm sand nearer to the sea. And so it began all over again. To their left the surf broke, edging ever nearer as the day wore on. The wind continued to gain momentum, buffeting their flanks. On and on they loped. The sky became a seething mass of heavy low-slung clouds. The wind cut them as it blew in off the sea which had now lost its diamonds. The incessant din of the crashing surf and the moaning wind hypnotised them as they swallowed the ground, mile after weary mile.

The day was drawing to a close when Marsha spotted something interesting ahead, the tall dark trunks of the Scots pines towering skywards away to their right. Their presence spoke to him of one thing, fresh water. Packo saw the trees, and drew the same conclusion.

They came to a deep gorge, the flow of water three hares' length. They waded in and gulped eagerly. It was like an elixir, golden and tantalising. Marsha stooped and allowed the water to flow over him. Its coldness revitalised and replenished him. Packo, his thirst quenched, stood still, his legs immersed in the flowing cold. He held his head askance as if listening to some strange silent voice. His eyes narrowed and he shivered. Marsha looked at him.

'Anything wrong?' he asked.

'Something is,' Packo answered, his voice a whisper, 'but I'm not sure what. There is evil here. My instinct is to run, to escape. Yet, for some reason, we have to stay.'

'Is this then the danger Horeb warned us about?' Marsha scanned the surrounding land, the tall Scots pines, the deep, heavily eroded gorge, the rushing water; did these contain some hidden danger?

'We must wait and face whatever is here,' Packo said.

Marsha nodded fatalistically. 'There's one good thing anyway,' he said, 'fresh water must provide fresh grass. Come on, let's go and eat.'

They advanced up the gorge and chose a spot where green shoots sprouted from the ground. Both hares ate, appreciating the succulence after the recent diet of coarse marram grass. On either side of them rugged, stony banks climbed steeply to where the Scots pines patrolled the land. The day's journey ached in their limbs as they climbed one of the steep banks. Once the gurgling water was behind them silence descended like a pall obscuring the outside world. They threaded their way through thorny gorse bushes, their yellow raiment loud in the sombre surroundings, and emerged in a clearing, a small, flat area, completely confined by the gorse bushes. There was an exit directly in front of them.

'We'll scoop out a form,' Marsha suggested, 'we can merge into the scenery.'

Packo did not argue, it was the sensible thing to do. Yet, he feared that wherever they rested in this perversely tranquil place, someone would know.

They huddled together as the sky darkened. The prevailing wind drove before it the ponderous rain-besotted clouds whose coming Horeb had predicted. As the hares crouched, ears pinned against their backs, the first heavy drops began to fall. There was a methodical resonance in their pit-patting. They struck the ground, tiny thuds spaced between split seconds of time. Slowly, the crescendo began to build, the thuds merging into a cacophony. Soon the shallow depression filled with water, accentuating their misery. 'This was not one of my smarter ideas,' Marsha growled.

Packo smiled in his adversity. 'Maybe not. It's hard to be perfect all the time.'

'Hmm. It's not just the discomfort. We could both put up with that. Perhaps your earlier warning about danger is getting to me. But look, we came here through the gorse bushes and found this small clearing. It appeared to be safe. We're surrounded on all sides by gorse, who is going to get to us here? No, it's this water I don't like. It's as if . . .'

He fell silent. The truth struck him. He clawed away the top sand and discovered thick, clinging clay. His eyes narrowed.

'What is it?' Packo asked, astonished at Marsha's behaviour.

'This is a trap, cleverly set to lure such as us on a night such as this. Water should escape from here, dissolve through the sand, find its own way to the gorge. It's time we got out of here.'

A loud, eerie cackle pierced the night, cutting through both them and the wild wind. Marsha advanced cautiously and peered into the darkness.

'Excellent, excellent,' a shrill voice piped. 'Every storm brings new playmates, and this time, it would appear, intelligent ones. Excellent!'

There were four of them. Marsha retreated. 'Grey squirrels on a night out,' he whispered to Packo.

Packo was stunned. This was not a usual habitat for greys. One would expect reds here, so near the sea and among the pines.

'A renegade band,' Marsha said, reading Packo's thoughts. 'Nasty lot; grey squirrels kill the reds and take over. Let's see what the situation is like to the rear.'

He stepped past Packo and squeezed into the gorse. Four more greys were stationed there. He retreated once again.

'Well! Four to the front, four to the rear. You can bet your life there is no other way out. They have us penned. Their teeth and claws can do us much harm.'

'We need weapons,' Packo spoke. He seemed almost nonchalant.

'Yes, but what? Where?'

'The very thing they have used to make our stay here so unpleasant, the clay. Quick, start digging it up, bank it towards the two exits.'

Marsha stared, mystified.

'Do it,' Packo urged. 'I'll take the front, you the rear.'

They worked frantically. The water continued to rise: obviously the squirrels knew that sooner or later the hares would be forced out. They were content to bide their time. Marsha and Packo pulled the clay out with their forepaws and pushed it behind them with their hind legs, building a wall which separated them from their foes. As they worked at the sloppy mud and dug deeper and deeper the water began to cover them completely. They strove on and just when it appeared that they would have to stop, the water suddenly began to drain away. They might well have heard the gurgling had it not been for the furore of the wind. They had removed the clay and the water had found its natural outlet.

'Packo, you're a genius. I would never have thought that that might happen.'

'Neither would I,' Packo replied honestly.

'Hey! What have we been doing then, banking up this clay?'

'Well, my original idea was . . .'

As time passed the squirrels became impatient. This was their game and they knew from the severity of the elements that their trap must be well and truly filled with water by now. The victims should be miserable and easy prey as they sought to escape. It always happened that way. Yet, they made no show. Was something wrong?

'They should 'ave bin out ages ago, boss,' one of the younger squirrels confronted his leader. ''Bout time we went in, that's wha' I think.'

'I'll do the thinking,' the boss replied. Yet, he was concerned. Had these hares somehow escaped undetected?

'Perraps you don't 'ave the bottle anymore.' That came from an older, battle-scarred squirrel, 'Perraps we should see if you've got what it takes.' This squirrel, Scarface, was not known for his patience.

The boss hesitated. Nothing like this had ever happened before, those trapped always came out. Something had gone wrong. He thought frantically. He had to reassert his authority. However, events began to overtake him.

'Afraid to come and get us are you?' The voice boomed above the storm. 'Greys, a right bunch of cowards when it comes to the crunch. Well, we're quite happy to wait here. We're warm and dry and sheltered from the wind and rain while you lot get washed out of it.' Marsha tried to sound relaxed as he taunted his adversaries. He wanted to goad them into action. It worked.

Scarface took the initiative. 'Right, that's it. Young Crasher, shoot round the other side, tell 'em we're goin' in. You've got fifteen seconds. Move it.'

Young Crasher shot off, his speed typifying the lightning

reflexes squirrels can achieve over short distances. Scarface started counting.

'Something is wrong here,' the boss said, intuitively aware that somehow the tables had been turned.

'Leave it out,' Scarface told him, 'we're goin' in.'

Young Crasher had not returned. The boss stood back while Scarface and another squirrel braced themselves. They moved forward. Marsha watched them approach. Packo did likewise to the rear. He had four to contend with.

Suddenly Marsha shouted, 'Strike.' The two hares began kicking the wet, clinging mud with their hind legs. A large dollup struck Scarface on the snout.

'Wha' the . . .' As he raised his head, another, larger dollop blinded him. The clay was spraying everywhere, covering everything, reducing the squirrels to leaden pugilists.

Packo was gleeful. 'Great experience for them,' he shouted as he aimed rhythmical powerful kicks at the wall of clay behind him.

Marsha picked his moment. 'Now,' he yelled. He jumped forward and caught Scarface with a mighty blow to the head. Packo was alongside him in a flash and delivered an unmerciful punch into the other squirrel's right flank. The sodden squirrels sank into oblivion. The nightmare they had dreamed up for others had suddenly become their own.

'Now, let's get out of here,' Marsha grinned. He thrust forward to the outer edge of the gorse bushes. He stopped in his tracks. The sight which met him was not a welcome one. He could have kicked himself. He had counted the squirrels earlier, he knew that there were eight of them. He had presumed that the majority must have gone to the rear. Presumed! He had broken one of his own cardinal rules. Never, in a tight corner, presume anything.

The boss's eyes darted to and fro. Young Crasher, his message delivered, had returned. Now the two squirrels lay in wait for their victims.

'So, hare, you have come at last, come to savour my sharp

claws, my nut cracking teeth. I shall enjoy sinking them into you.' The boss was delighted with himself. His leadership had been vindicated, and Young Crasher would act as witness.

'Move out,' Packo urged, 'the squirrels from the rear are beginning to come through.'

Marsha hesitated. He barely had room to make a jump of any consequence, most of his body was hemmed in by the thick gorse. If he tried anything the squirrel would be on him in a flash and the wounds he would receive would be fearsome. Yet, he realised that he would have to take his chance. There were four squirrels to the rear, recovering quickly, and probably hopping mad too! He took a deep breath and was on the point of leaping forth when the totally unexpected happened. A huge, dark shape emerged from the night and landed squarely on top of the boss, winding him and very nearly forcing the darting eyes from their sockets. In an instant Marsha recognised him. It was Fatso. Young Crasher was paralysed with fear. Marsha rushed out, hit him a resounding blow on the snout ensuring that even on this night he saw a few stars, and called to the two hares, 'Down to the beach and don't delay.'

Packo glanced at Fatso. 'Took you long enough,' he laughed. The three hares loped away, back to the seashore and the frothy waves.

Chapter Ten

The wind tore through the water causing the waves to race, rise, and finally crash upon the shore. The white, spitting foam was a venomous testament to the fury of the ocean. The three hares broke from the relative calm of the sand dunes to the explosion at the sea front. It represented the glorious sound of freedom and they raced hard until the place of ordeal was a mere dot against the dark and heavy sky. Marsha led them behind a sand dune where they squatted among the marram grasses. They were sheltered from the wind, the sea's spray, and the worst of the rain. A collective mirth descended on them.

'Nasty bunch, those squirrels,' Packo said.

'Yes,' Marsha agreed, 'and we certainly owe you a debt of gratitude for saving us from at the very least a mauling, and possibly even death. Thank you.'

Marsha looked directly at Fatso. Suddenly he realised that they did not even know his name. 'What can we call you?' he asked simply.

Fatso appeared embarrassed. 'Well, my name is Lotto.'

'Lotto!' Marsha and Packo spoke simultaneously.

The fat hare smiled coyly. 'I was always a bit on the big side,' he explained. 'As a leveret my mother used to say that I had the appetite of a complete litter.' He fell silent.

'You were the one I saw following us,' Marsha stated.

Lotto nodded.

'Why did you do that?'

'It was the old hare,' Lotto said.

'The old hare?' Packo asked. 'You mean Horeb with whom we spent the night?'

'Horeb?' Lotto was genuinely mystified.

'You remember Litrel, the hare whose group you terrorised?' Packo persisted.

Lotto hung his head in shame. 'I remember,' he muttered.

'Well, he took us to see an old hare, Horeb.'

'Yes, I did see that old hare at a distance. But no, that's not the one I'm referring to. This one came to me at night, the very night I was made outcast. He was very old, grey about the whiskers and he had sort of "timeless" eyes.'

'Timeless eyes,' Packo repeated the words slowly. 'The Purveyor.' He glanced towards Marsha. Lotto had seen the hare who had encouraged them after their journey through the forest.

'And what did this hare say to you?' Marsha asked.

'Well,' Lotto began, hesitating as if he was unable to find the right words to express himself, 'initially, he didn't say anything. He just gazed at me. I was sore, you two gave me a hefty kick each, and then some more.' He smiled as he remembered their first encounter. 'I deserved that. Anyway, as he looked at me, or, more correctly, looked through me, my life seemed to . . . to peel away. For the first time I was able to see myself as others see me. It was quite extraordinary! What I saw was ugly. You see, as I've told you, I was always big. When I first ventured from my form and met other hares, they treated me with a certain amount of trepidation. I used this to assert myself. I threw my weight around a bit, gathered a gang around me, became a bully.

'When that old hare gazed into my eyes that night he somehow made me see myself. I saw a corrupt and wasted life. I saw myself as one without a friend, ever, only groups of hangers on who were content to feed off the fear I instilled in others. I saw myself as one to be pitied, not feared. I ached and asked simply, "What must I do?"

'The old hare smiled, a kindly smile, and said, "It's never too late, fate always throws a lifeline. I am fate, and now I throw you that lifeline. If you wish to redeem your life, follow the two hares who stood up to you. Do not join them immediately, you will know the time."

' "And what can I expect?" I asked him. "You can expect to suffer in a titanic struggle; you can expect sacrifice. Through your sacrifice you will learn the wisdom of love; in that wisdom you will find redemption." Do you know, the words are burned into my mind. The problem is, I don't understand them.

'So, I followed you. Now, that was suffering! You travel so quickly. I found it difficult to keep up, especially with my sides still a little sore. Actually, I thought that I had lost you. I wandered into that cluster of trees seeking shelter, as I suppose you did. When I arrived the squirrels were gathered around that thicket of gorse bushes, so I waited. I heard you taunting them. I have no idea what caused me to intervene when I did. It was as if that old hare was beside me. "Go for it," he said, so I did. I landed on top of that squirrel and heard his lungs explode. You know the rest.'

Lotto finished his account. He had spoken throughout in a quiet, unassuming tone. 'I've got a lot to learn,' he said, 'will you have me?'

'We don't know exactly where we're going, or what to expect if ever we reach our destination,' Marsha told him honestly. 'We've been in mortal danger twice already, we can't offer you an easy time of it.'

'I'm willing to take my chances, and I'll make sure that you won't regret having me. I've been given the opportunity to do something worthwhile with my life, something I've never achieved in the past.'

Packo broke in, understanding Lotto's feelings. 'All three of us must attempt to find the "Land of Deep Shadow", only there will we find answers to our questions.'

'I can join you then?'

'You can join us,' Marsha and Packo echoed.

'Great,' Lotto shouted, 'great. Let's get going then.'

'Not so fast,' Marsha chuckled. 'It's wet, blowing a gale, and thoroughly unpleasant out there. Let's dig in, rest until daybreak, and then move on.'

Lotto seemed pleased. He scraped out a shallow depression and rested his large frame. His eyes were gleaming. Marsha and Packo did likewise. Lotto's arrival made them both feel much more comfortable.

Dawn broke, bright and blustery. The heavy rain clouds had passed and patches of blue smiled between the white stratos clouds which travelled the sky. The three hares munched the marram grass, chewing the slightly more succulent shoots near to the base. It was hardly heady fare but it would sustain them through the coming day's journey. They felt reluctant to move. It seemed that they were no nearer their destination and their experience of the previous night weighed heavily on them. Their journey had proved fraught with danger. That, in itself, was not the problem. A hare's life often hangs by a thread; fleeing from trouble is par for the course. Yet now, on this journey, they seemed to be courting trouble. Why? And how far had they travelled? They were many days from their starting point. But, in terms of their destination, how far had they come? Doubts surfaced. Were they really only chasing a dream?

Suddenly Marsha looked up and found Packo staring at him. 'I know,' Packo said, 'I'd turn back now, get on with the rest of our lives, forget this fanciful adventure. Yet, that hare we watched die, that broken body, that piteous plea; that was all real. We have to go on, even if it takes us the rest of our lives, we have to go on.'

'Oh, I know that deep down,' Marsha smiled. 'It's just that I wish we had some idea of how long, how far. Not knowing is the worst thing. When you don't know, you doubt.'

'I can't explain this to you, Marsha,' Packo answered, 'but I know that we are going somewhere. Come, let's feel the sand shift beneath our paws, let's meet this new day, and whatever it might bring.'

Marsha grinned. 'You know, the worst knowledge we could possess would be to know our destiny. Live today, let tomorrow come if it will! Let's get down to that beach and get moving.'

Lotto was shuffling around. His sleep had been fitful, excited as he was by the prospect of his new adventure. Now, when the time came to move, he felt he needed rest. He was used to sleeping late. Old habits die hard.

'Time to move, Lotto,' Marsha advised him.

'Oh, er, right, fine.' He attempted to sound enthusiastic. The night's excitement is often lost in the pale, early dawn.

Marsha led them over the sand dune and down the soft sandy slope to the beach. He headed for the sea line and reached a point from which the sea had receded earlier. There he felt the ground firmer underfoot. He turned to his right and began at an easy pace. He maintained it until the sun had passed its zenith. He kept a watchful eye on Lotto who was travelling at his shoulder. He appeared comfortable enough. Running to a hare is as natural as breathing.

It was mid afternoon when Marsha decided to see what Lotto had in him. He began to stride out. He increased the speed gradually until the wind streamed along their bodies and the sand flashed beneath them. Now the trio were really moving. A thousand paces, two, three, four, and Marsha continued to push on. His head was tucked in, his eyes alert to the terrain all around him. Packo was to the rear; he would take care of that area. By the occasional rotation of his pupils Marsha was able to check on Lotto. He was keeping up remarkably well for such a large hare. Five, six, seven, eight thousand paces. Still Lotto was there. Marsha was impressed. Despite his weight, Lotto could move when he had to. It was a comforting thought. Then, something ahead caught Marsha's attention.

Directly in front of them the sun gleamed against grey. Rocks! They had been running quickly, now they joined the wind itself. They streaked across the damp sand faster and faster. Marsha caught a clear view of the land and the exact shape it was taking. Without warning he began to curve inland. Lotto, surprised by the slight change in direction, suddenly found himself four paces adrift. He grunted as he strained to make up the leeway.

Packo had observed what lay ahead and realised that Marsha would lead them inland. He was ready when the sudden change in direction came and he found himself in front of Lotto. He followed Marsha into the sand dunes, the final short ascent enough to curb their speed as they pulled up just over the brow. They were both breathing hard when Lotto appeared, powering towards them. He shrieked and jumped, avoiding a collision by a matter of inches, and came to an abrupt halt in soft sand, his legs completely disappearing. He lay still, his heart pounding, his lungs gasping eagerly for breath. As he lay there, his vast bulk stretched across the sand, he felt the first drops of rain patting heavily into his pelt. He cast an eye around and saw Marsha and Packo grinning at him.

'I thought I was going to die,' he said, his breathing still irregular.

'I thought you were going to take us with you,' Marsha laughed, the exertion of the recent run not evident in his voice.

'I didn't know that you were going to stop so abruptly. At least I managed to fling myself into the air.'

'Good job too,' Packo joked, 'you might have crushed us both.'

'Sorry about that,' Lotto apologised.

'Not at all, not at all,' Marsha passed it off. 'In future I shall attempt to give you adequate notice of abrupt halts.'

'And why change direction?' Lotto asked.

'Ah, well, you should have known about that,' Marsha told him.

Lotto's eyes widened. How could he have known?

'We were running out of beach,' Packo informed him, reading his thoughts by means of his astonished expression.

'Cliffs, up ahead, we're going to have to climb around them. And that's not all,' Marsha continued, 'we're in for a bit of foul weather too. We'll take a breather and then we'll try to find some shelter for the night.'

Lotto nodded and lay quietly. Marsha studied him. He had purposely set the very fast pace, and Lotto had done very well.

All he needed was to shed some of his excess weight, develop and tone his muscles, particularly his hind quarters which were overburdened with flabby flesh. A week's exercise similar to today's should see to that. A physically fit Lotto could prove to be an invaluable asset. He was taller, when sitting on his hind legs, than Marsha or Packo. Marsha was an average sized hare, a little over eight pounds in weight. Lotto was easily eleven pounds. His paw pads were thick; this, allied to his bulk, meant that he could be an outstanding fighter. Marsha speculated that he wasn't. Lotto had probably never been in a tight corner, his size would have seen to that. Occasionally he might have delivered a telling blow. It would have been more by chance than design. Brute force is rarely enough, technique is the crucial factor. Lotto needed to be taught how to use his strength, how to deliver that telling blow by using both his strength and his weight. He needed to learn how to defend himself, and when to avoid a fight rather than risk injury. He needed to know where to deliver the blow. He had experienced first hand what a good kick to the rib cage can do. Marsha would ensure that he knew where the other vulnerable areas were, eyes, ears, back of the ears, snout, heart. And he would try to teach him the most important rule of all; a creature who doesn't threaten you must be left in peace.

Suddenly Marsha pricked his ears. He heard noise away to his right. Packo also heard it. The rain was heavier now, the wind had freshened. Then, there was the sound again. A snort, short and belligerent. Trouble!

Like a figure in a dream moving slowly and without purpose, a fox trotted into the hare's shelter. Marsha and Packo watched him, fascinated, unable to react. The fox snorted again, blinked, and looked up. When he saw them he seemed as surprised as they. He had been seeking some respite from the rain. He had not been concentrating on finding a dinner. Now, he was not about to refuse one.

Lotto had been very nearly asleep. His legs were still buried in sand, his body prostrate. The fox was very near but Lotto had gone undetected. The fox's attention had been drawn to Marsha and Packo. Lotto now became alert — that snort was familiar. As a leveret he had been chased by a fox, it had nearly cost him his life. He had escaped only because the fox had become entangled in a snare. It was then that he had become familiar with the snorts and shrieks of the wretched animal. He had wanted to help but he was too frightened. He watched the fox struggle, entangle himself further, and eventually die. And here was another fox, not three paces from him. The moment seemed endless. The rain no longer existed, nor the wind. There was nothing save the fox, standing leering; and Marsha and Packo, rigid, shocked, overawed.

'Woweee.'

Lotto shouted above the storm, shattering the spell. The fox turned, startled eyes wide open. Using all his strength Lotto drove his hind legs through the sand and sent a huge spray directly into the fox's eyes, blinding him, the grit irritating his pupils, flaming his nostrils, filling his open mouth. He whined and shook his head frantically.

'This way,' Marsha commanded, stung into action by the unexpected events. The three hares fled the scene, heading for the rocks and the higher ground.

The fox howled and opened his eyes. Mad rage removed his smarting pain. His vengeance would be mighty. The fox was in no hurry. He was privy to information which obviously the hares did not possess. They were climbing to the top of the rocks, to the Chaos Chasm. There they would have to turn back, there he would wreak his terrible revenge. The fox grunted, a deep, self-satisfied grunt. Patience, yes patience, his time would come.

Marsha raced across the remaining sand dunes. Packo and Lotto followed at the same frenetic speed. Packo took his customary position at the rear, continually scouring the land behind for a sign of the fox. There was none.

The evening continued to darken and the rain hurled its fury at them. The wind, cross in both course and character, tore and buffeted their bodies. As he stepped on to the rocks Marsha felt them wet and greasy underfoot. He realised that they must slow down. But the fox would eventually have to slacken his pace too, conditions were the same for both prey and predator. They began to climb, moving in a criss-cross pattern, hopping nimbly from one rock to the next. Marsha plotted their course, Lotto concentrated all his attention to the task at hand, while Packo continued his surveillance of the rear. Still no sign of the fox.

Now the climb became steeper. Marsha was forced to slow down yet again, forced to pick his steps ever more gingerly. Finally the summit was reached. A plateau stretched out in front of them. Marsha strode forward. He had stepped no more than five paces when he stopped, horror etched across his face. He was staring into the Chaos Chasm! He edged closer and pressed himself hard against the rock. A great gap yawned. He estimated that it was five hares' length across. And it was deep. He edged closer to the brink. Far, far below, the crashing sea, white and foamy, broke upon the rocks. The wind whistled and moaned like a lost demented soul. Over on the other side of the gap a great, wet, black slab of smooth rock faced him. It was slightly higher than the side they now occupied. That did not help.

Packo stepped to Marsha's side. 'The Chaos Chasm.'

'Yes,' Marsha agreed, 'The Chaos Chasm. What an apt name on a night like this. We could not have chosen a worse time to arrive, foul weather and an angry assailant behind us. Let's get it over with.'

They retreated to the edge of the flat rock. Marsha gazed hard but found it almost impossible to see the gap. Dark against dark. Lotto's eyes were bulging. 'We've got to . . . jump it, haven't we?'

Marsha grinned displaying his usual style. 'Hey, big fellow, that jump is no problem. You could do it in your sleep. Just run to the edge, leap, and aim to land as high on that rock over there as you possibly can. Watch!'

Marsha raced forward and sprang across the black divide. His heart beat wildly, he was terrified. His words had been nothing more than bravado. They had to get across. That's all there was to it. He landed on the black slab of rock, managing to reach the topmost lip. Behind him lay the slope, wet and slippery, all too ready to deliver victims to the breakers below. He dragged himself up.

'Right, Lotto,' he shouted across, 'A good long jump, and keep your eyes open!'

'Go, Lotto,' Packo urged, 'don't land on Marsha!'

Lotto glanced at him and then raced forward. He was some feet from the Chaos Chasm when he launched himself, pushing off with a mighty thrust of his hind legs. Like an enormous black bird he flew over the chasm and landed with a resounding thud well beyond where Marsha stood watching. A great smile spread across his face. 'Come on, Packo,' he yelled gleefully, 'piece of cake.'

Packo leaned back to begin his run. Suddenly, his eye caught a movement to his right. The fox was approaching the edge of the precipice, leering. His strategy had paid off handsomely. He had not bothered to follow the hares, rather he had skirted the base of the crags and then climbed the steeper, eastern side. He had actually arrived at the Chaos Chasm before the hares. There he had changed his plan. He deduced that they would imagine that he was following. Therefore they would not turn back. No, they would attempt to jump across. So, he had waited for the first two to disappear. They were out of the way now. This last one would be his prize.

As soon as the other two hares had landed on the far side the fox showed himself. He moved out of his place of concealment and stood at the edge of the divide, directly in front of Packo. Packo had one chance, and that chance must be taken now.

He raced forward until he was almost within snapping distance of the fox. He pushed himself off. The fox watched in savage fury as his prey flew past. Packo landed. Marsha and Lotto cheered. But he was short of the safety of the crag's lip. He was on the giant slab of flat rock, and he began to slide, slowly and inexorably, towards the Chaos Chasm and the two-hundred-foot drop to the sharp rocks and frothy sea.

Chapter Eleven

The rain, driven by the wind's fury, surged in massive sheets. The sky, dark and full of threats, was a huge canopy of death. Above all the din and storm-tossed noise, a mighty roll of rumbling thunder shattered the heavens and a streak of white hot lightning whipped the earth, momentarily illuminating the entire bizarre scene.

Packo frantically tried to hold on. He buckled his hind legs beneath his body and felt his bones jarring on the hard rock. His forepaws were splayed in front of him as he tried to maximise his body contact with the slippery slope. His fall towards the chasm was slow and excruciating. He was sliding to his doom.

The fox, standing on the other side of the divide, savoured every moment. His prey had escaped him, but now he was witness to an exquisite drama. The taste of warm flesh would not be his, but he would feel amply avenged when the hare finally slid to the crashing sea. He sat and waited patiently. He prided himself on his good sense not to attempt the jump. The first two hares had been lucky. This third one, a young, well developed specimen, would pay the ultimate price for his folly. And he, the fox, had a front seat view. Wonderful!

Packo wondered what he could do. Occasionally the tiniest irregularity afforded him a brief moment of purchase and the slipping was contained. But his body weight would pull him down, render him unable to take advantage of the minute opportunities fate presented. He remained calm, fully aware of his predicament, fully appreciative that if he tried to stand or became frantic, he would disappear over the edge in double fast time. Yet the edge was approaching ever nearer and when his hind legs suddenly lost contact with the rock and flailed aimlessly in mid-air, he realised that all was lost. There was no way he could climb, no way he could simply hang on. This was the end. He thought of his mother. How he had enjoyed her warmth and comfort on those nightly visitations! They were as real and vivid to him now as if she was there beside him.

He had not achieved much in his brief life and now it seemed his quest for the Land of Deep Shadow was passing from him.

He slipped a little further. It seemed that he must topple over the terrible brink but, somehow, he still managed to cling on.

'Packo, Packo, take it in your mouth. Take it!' It was Marsha screaming above the nightmare.

'Take what? Take what?' he thought. 'What? Where?'

He moved his head frantically. He slipped further. Half of him now hung precariously in mid air. His weight was thrown forward on to his forepaws, his body bent at a ninety degree angle.

Again Marsha screamed at him. 'The line, Packo, to your left. The line.'

He caught sight of it. A long, thick, ivy tendril torn from a tree. There it was. His last chance. Now he would have to gather his courage and make a grab for it.

He yanked his head and grabbed for the ivy. As he did so he toppled backwards and disappeared over the edge. He had taken the chance and plunged into the Chaos Chasm.

The fox jumped and shrieked with delight as he watched Packo plunge over the precipice. Marsha stood rigid, horrified, not wanting to believe. Packo was the Seer, the one called to the Land of Deep Shadow. If either was destined to reach that land, surely it was Packo? It was all over now, the great quest was finished.

He turned to retreat further up the crags, away from the shattering scene.

Lotto was there. He was not the forlorn heap Marsha expected to see. He held the tendril between his teeth and, by means of all his considerable strength, he was pulling the life-line up, moving methodically backwards step by step. Marsha's heart missed a beat. He rushed over and grabbed the woody ivy between his teeth, biting hard into it. He fell into step with Lotto. Suddenly Packo's forepaws appeared on the rock, then his head. He had grasped the ivy firmly, his jaws locked shut. Now most of his body was on the slab and finally his hindquarters touched the hard rock. He was managing to scramble up the slippery slab. Marsha and Lotto continued to pull, their necks extended. Not far now, just a little more, a little more.

The fox had watched it all, disgusted. Not only had he lost his supper, he had lost the satisfaction of knowing that no one else would ever enjoy the feed this hare would provide. He was furious; he leapt the Chaos Chasm. He landed to Packo's right, level with him. His jowls dripped, his murderous eyes shone.

Marsha and Lotto tugged harder. Packo was near to safety now, surely he was not going to be taken at the last moment?

The fox lurched to his left, his sharp teeth snapping vehemently. As he moved to within inches of Packo he stumbled backwards screaming shrilly. Packo reached safety and turned just as the fox, groping frantically, slipped the final few feet to his doom. The Chaos Chasm swallowed him, welcoming its latest victim, a victim of his own insatiable greed.

'Well,' Packo gasped, 'thanks, the two of you.'

'Lotto deserves the credit,' Marsha said, 'I don't know where he found that ivy, but he had the good sense to cling on to it even after you had disappeared. To be honest, I thought you were a goner.'

Packo turned towards the big hare. 'Thanks Lotto. I'm certainly glad you came along, I owe you.'

'Oh, you owe me nothing,' Lotto replied shuffling awkwardly, 'I'm just pleased you're all right and that I could be useful.' He shook himself, spraying them and a substantial area with fine drops of water. The rain seemed to be abating and the sky was brightening. It might yet be a fine evening. The hares hardly noticed.

'So, where did you find that ivy?' Marsha asked.

'Up beyond the crags. See those pine trees up there?' Lotto pointed vaguely to a spot where the ground levelled and two forlorn-looking trees grew against all odds. It was difficult to know whether they were alive or dead. Their trunks were bent landwards, the result of the constant buffeting of the wind off the sea.

'Actually, it was lying at the foot of one of them, almost as if it had been left there purposely.'

Marsha and Packo glanced at one another. Perhaps it had!

'I don't even know where the idea came from. Suddenly I felt myself drawn in that direction. I saw the ivy and brought it here. To tell you the truth, Packo, when you disappeared over the edge I thought that you had plunged to your death. Yet, I couldn't let go of the line. Then, just after you had fallen, I felt the strain. I knew then that you had managed to grasp it.'

'I only managed to grasp it after I had toppled over,' Packo admitted, 'it's fortunate it was good and long. Someone out there continues to look out for us.'

'I merely placed the suggestion in Lotto's mind, he deserves great credit for the way in which he responded.'

The voice was calm, full of warmth, reassuring. It had a dream-like quality.

The hares jumped round and there, standing against the brightening skyline, his back to the ocean, was the old hare.

'Who are you?' Marsha asked.

'Just a guide of sorts, an adviser to some extent, nothing more. Now, you must change direction. Head east into the rising sun. It has been ordained that you must cross the Great Wilderness! See, it is over there.' He pointed and, as if in a trance, all three hares stared into the gloom.

'What can you tell us about it?' Marsha asked, turning back. The old hare had vanished.

'Where did he go?' Lotto was astounded.

'Don't ask,' Marsha replied, 'he seems to be able to appear and disappear at will.'

'I'm sure he was the one who told me to follow you,' Lotto said, 'but I can't be sure. I never was very good with faces.'

'He was the one all right,' Packo told him.

'Let's get out of here,' Marsha suggested.

The three hares, picking their steps carefully on the craggy plateau, began to travel in the newly appointed direction. It wasn't long before the rocks started to drop away. Marsha hesitated. He looked round. Far off on the horizon the sun shone in shafts through gaps in the clouds. The ocean twinkled burnished gold, an ever changing vastness. How he loved it! How he longed to stay and feel its freshness, to race the waves again as they broke upon the shore, to experience the wind-blown spray. As he turned, reluctantly, to begin the descent, his heart ached. He knew that he would never view the great sea again.

Descending the rocks proved to be much more hazardous than ascending. The temptation was to move too quickly, to be pulled downwards and lose control. The crags petered out giving way to a long scree slope. Its incline was severe at first, but then, as they approached the bottom, it became gentler. Finally they stepped on to level ground scattered with short clumps of grass. The evening sun sprinkled them red. Very soon it would disappear.

'I don't know about you two,' Marsha said, 'but I'm beginning to feel that some rest is in order. Let's eat and then find a safe form.'

His suggestion was accepted passively. They nibbled, uninterestedly, at the short blades of grass. They settled into a shallow depression among stones, their brown coats blending perfectly with their surroundings. They fell into a dreamless sleep.

It was late when they awoke the following morning. Marsha was surprised that he had slept so long, and a little annoyed with himself too. Darkness had helped camouflage them. In daylight discovery would have been much easier.

The morning was warm, the sky an immaculate blue, the air motionless. The huge outcrop behind them acted as a shield, keeping the sea breezes at bay. Marsha studied the landscape. The summit from which they had descended was the beginning of a long range of mountains which stretched northwards. The rocky plateau on which they had stood was very high above them. To the south the sand dunes bordered the land that lay before them. That land, to the east, the direction they must now take, looked like an endless, flat area. This was the Great Wilderness! It was not inviting.

Marsha heard a groan beside him and saw Packo open his eyes, smile, and flash his white teeth.

'I know,' he said, 'I know. Time to move on.'

Marsha nodded.

Packo gave Lotto a nudge. He woke instantly.

'Sorry,' he apologised, 'I hope I did not detain you. Ready to move?'

'You didn't detain us,' Marsha assured him, 'and yes, we're ready to move, unless either of you feels like eating first.'

Packo shrugged, Lotto followed his example. They could always stop somewhere and find something.

Marsha did not force the pace. The vast landscape ahead of them represented a long, rigorous journey. This stage was a marathon, not a sprint. The sun rose higher and higher until it reached its zenith and beat down upon them. The land was a patchy green. There was no great hardship to be endured and, although Marsha did consider calling a halt, he felt comfortable enough to continue. He checked Lotto at his shoulder and noticed that he too had plenty in reserve. On and on they drove until finally, when the sun was casting long shadows in front of them, Marsha stopped. He had chosen a green area, having observed during the day that such sources of food were becoming more scarce.

They nibbled casually, their throats dry. They found a safe place to sleep, and settled down. The following morning Marsha was awake before the sun rose. He prodded Packo and Lotto.

'Let's eat before the sun rises and evaporates the dew. And eat well,' he advised, 'today we might well discover what the Great Wilderness is all about.'

They munched the short grass, cool and succulent while the dew still clung to it. The new day's sun peeped up over the far horizon as they began again. Another day's journey into the endless terrain. As they travelled their surroundings took on an almost surreal appearance. The ground became harder beneath their paws, the only growth prickly, green plants with thick stems. Marsha had never seen their kind before and avoided them. That night they found nothing to eat. The following two nights they fared no better. Each day it became hotter and hotter. The ground became coarser and bit into their paw pads. They were surrounded by a bleakness and emptiness which gnawed into their spirits. Worst of all, there was no end in sight. After four days of travelling they were surrounded by an infinity of barrenness, save for the presence of the green plants. Marsha probed them and discovered that their thick stems were hard and covered with sharp needles which jutted out to prevent a close examination.

They discovered too that the searing heat of the day gave way to a piercing cold at night. It was so cold that sleep did not come easily. It was Packo who suggested that they should conserve their energy by resting while the sun was at its cruellest. They travelled at night, the stars speckling the heavens their guide. This they did for two nights but now they moved at a fraction of their ordinary speed. They were weakened by hunger, racked by stomach pains, their paw pads scuffed and sore. While they rested during the heat of the day, they continued to suffer. Shady areas were scant. The larger prickly plants cast a small shadow and then virtually none when the sun bore down on them from its highest point in the sky.

Marsha became more and more concerned. He was suffering from periods of dizziness and lightheadedness, a result of dehydration. His mouth was dry, his voice hoarse. His rib cage showed through his pelt and his paw pads were cracked and smeared with congealed blood. He saw his own deteriorating condition reflected in Packo and Lotto. Lotto in particular was suffering. His excess weight had quickly disappeared — too quickly. His skin hung loose and his strength had evaporated. Through all of his suffering he never complained. He trudged on at Marsha's shoulder, head down, his breathing raucous, every step a battle. His resolution shone through. He had become, in every sense, the true hare.

Marsha racked his brain. Surely there was something he could do, something. But what? The wilderness engulfed them, its vastness hemming them in, confining them. It was a prison every bit as real as a cage. Thoughts that he had lost his way plagued him. Was he only succeeding in leading them in ever decreasing circles? Yet, despite his bouts of dizziness his mind was lucid enough. As for the lightheadedness, that only seemed to affect him during the heat of the day. He had maintained an exact easterly course, and even now, shuffling along as dawn broke on another day, he was as certain as he possibly could be that his course was straight and true. Packo and Lotto were behind, following silently. Despite his pain and discomfort, Marsha smiled. Every place has something good. The lovely quality of the Great Wilderness was the silence. It was constant. At the ocean it had been the continual hum and ripple of the waves. The silence here was as constant as the noise there. One can learn to relax in constancy.

Then, quite suddenly and for no apparent reason, Marsha jerked his head skywards. The sight which met his eyes was terrible to behold. A great golden eagle, the king of birds, was diving at them. His head was tucked, his wings shortened and held steady, his curved beak gleamed and his cold eyes flashed menace. He would be upon them in seconds.

Chapter Twelve

'Spread out, run for it,' Marsha shouted hoarsely. Too late.

Talons hung tantalisingly in the air and Lotto, unable to react quickly enough, suddenly felt them pierce his flanks. He yelled and automatically slumped to the ground. The eagle was young. He made to rise with his prey. He found that he couldn't. The great wings flapped, issuing a draught which created a cloud of dust. Lotto lay prone, spreading himself as far as possible over the ground. The eagle refused to yield. Realising the measure of his task he increased the speed of his flapping wings. Lotto's body began to rise.

Marsha and Packo had looked on, horrified, unable to move. It was all so unreal. Yet, their anger was rising. Packo saw again his sister Dersall, her body being lifted by the hawk. The spell was broken. He shot forward and, with every ounce of strength left in him, he hurtled himself at the great bird. He leapt twelve feet into the air and butted the eagle squarely on the body beneath one of the huge wings. The blow surprised and winded the bird, forcing him to release his load. Lotto fell to the ground with a thud. Marsha rushed towards him as the eagle spread his enormous wings and soared away. Packo crashed to the desert floor, his bones jarring on the hard ground.

'Quickly,' Marsha shouted urgently, 'get him under one of the prickly plants, it's our only chance.'

They tugged and pulled and cajoled and managed to deposit Lotto under one of the cacti. It was hardly a safe refuge. The eagle turned in a great arc. He was not finished yet. He gathered his strength for another assault. This time he decided to hunt one of the smaller hares. He came out of the rising sun, wings held in to avoid the spikes protruding from the plants. His talons were once more spread, his razor sharp beak ready to rip one of them apart. His eyes danced, enjoying the sight of three cowering hares.

Marsha looked up hopelessly. There was only one thing to do. He must attempt to divert the eagle's attention, lead him away so that the others might have a chance of survival. Packo was the one who must arrive at the Land of Deep Shadow. Perhaps this was to be Marsha's role, sacrificing himself to save Packo and Lotto. So be it. He darted from the scant protection of the cactus and stood, ready. The eagle eyed him. Just as he thought! He had so frightened one of them that he had run from cover. This one he would have no difficulty lifting, and he was far enough away from the cactus for that to present no problem. Then he realised that not all was as it should be. This hare was not cowering before him! Rather he was standing, waiting, knowing. Knowing what? Was that other one, the mad one, going to charge him again? He would give him no opportunity.

The eagle dropped from the sky, diving with the speed of a streak of lightning.

He was but a split second from contact when Marsha, with astonishing alacrity, feinted to one side. As the bird veered Marsha raced under his body. The eagle unfurled his wings, caught the updraught, and soared into the sky. His heart thumped, not from exertion, from excitement. This was a challenge to his obvious superiority. He caught sight of Marsha a hundred paces from his last position. He was standing still, watching, waiting, ready to try again to evade the kill.

The eagle felt a rush of frenzy break over him. He rounded upon his prey once more. Instinctively he came out of the low slung sun again, knowing that Marsha would have difficulty seeing him. This time he held his speed in check ensuring control of his movements. He anticipated Marsha's attempt to unbalance him and, by sheer good fortune, moved to the side Marsha had chosen.

Marsha had not expected the ploy to work a second time. Now, as he pushed off to his left he did not try to sidestep back.That was what the eagle expected. Instead he continued to run, racing from the grasping talons. Again the bird was frustrated. He had anticipated correctly but the hare had escaped. He veered to face the new direction. Marsha zig-zagged, changing direction with amazing turns of speed. The eagle was with him, following every move. It was only a matter of time, and Marsha knew it. Ahead he spotted some rocks, a broken outcrop which might provide some cover. Yet, it could only be a transitory hideout at best. If he went to earth the eagle might return for Packo and Lotto. He couldn't allow that to happen.

He reached the first rock and dashed behind it. The eagle saw him disappear. Now he knew the hare was trapped. He would drop down and pluck him out. His time had come. He changed the direction of his wings slightly so that they trapped the wind. He landed on the rock. Marsha was beneath him, exhausted.

The eagle fluttered his wings. This was the part he always enjoyed most. The kill, warm and satisfying, a moment of exquisite pleasure. Slowly he flapped the mighty wings and plunged at Marsha.

'Arrrrr . . .'

The strange noise exploded in the silence. The eagle glanced around and felt the blow strike the side of his head. The great wings fluttered briefly one last time, but somehow the power had deserted him. He collapsed, engulfed in blackness.

'Gotcha, yer great flamin' greasebag.' A thin, wiry hare was jumping up and down, delighted with himself.

'Ey, ey,' he shouted, 'come out, I bagged 'im.'

Marsha pushed himself up, hardly able to believe what was happening. The hare he saw for the first time was smaller than himself, thin and dishevelled.

'How?' Marsha asked.

'Wiv a rock. Always bin an expert. One of me many talents.

Lucky for you yer came this way.'

Marsha's eyes widened. 'But . . . I don't understand.'

'Simple innit? Greasebag comes down, I picked up a rock, jackpot! Dead as the proverbial dodo. A shot to be praad of!'

Marsha still wasn't quite with it but he was grateful. 'Well, thanks. But for your intervention I might have ended up as his supper. I've two friends back there, one of them is injured. We need a safe place to rest.'

'No problem, guv'nor, bring 'em 'ere, I've just the ticket. Better still, I'll cam wiv yer.'

Marsha nodded and without further ado he returned to Packo and Lotto.

'How is he?' Marsha asked Packo.

'Could have been a lot worse. The bleeding has stopped. Flesh wounds, he was lucky.'

'Can you travel a short distance?' Marsha asked Lotto.

'Yes, I'll manage. Sorry to be such a nuisance.'

'Big lad!' the wiry hare interjected.

'Yes,' Marsha replied. 'Oh, this is . . . , I'm sorry, I don't know your name.'

'Crust,' the smaller hare replied.

'Crust?' Marsha echoed.

'Yeah. Me ma used t' call me a tuf ole crust. It sorta stuck.'

'Anyway,' Marsha continued, 'this is Packo and Lotto.'

'Lotto must be the big lad,' Crust concluded.

'Correct,' Marsha answered succinctly, 'and I'm Marsha. Crust saved the day by killing the eagle.'

'How did he manage that?' Packo asked, eyeing the wily Crust with a new-found respect.

'Later,' Marsha told him. 'First, to safety. Ready, Lotto?'

'Yes, of course.' Lotto raised his still vast frame from which his flesh hung in limp layers. He was in obvious discomfort but he did not complain. He followed Marsha and Crust, each step an effort. The wounds along his flanks began to weep. Crust led them past the place of his triumphant throw to another cluster of rocks nearby. The narrow entrance caused Lotto some anguish.

Once inside, however, like the others, he marvelled. It was like a fortress. A flat, broad slab of rock rested overhead across the boulders. Even for four hares there was more than enough space.

'Them wounds need cleanin',' Crust advised. ''Ang about, I'll get somefink.'

He returned in next to no time carrying a large, succulent slice of yellowy green vegetation.

''Ere, rub it on.'

Marsha took it in both paws and squeezed the juice over the wounds, nimbly applying his paw to the injured areas. He worked silently for several minutes ensuring that each wound was thoroughly clean so that infection would not set in. By the time he had finished Lotto was already falling asleep. That was probably the best medicine of all. Marsha turned to talk to the others. They had disappeared! He became alarmed. Then he heard a thud. It was faint but he knew that he had not imagined it. He braced himself. He heard a grunt, a groan, another grunt.

Suddenly Packo burst into view, his eyes alight. He swivelled and disappeared into the exit again. Almost immediately his rear end re-emerged. His head, when it eventually came into view, was near the ground. He dragged a large chunk of the same type of vegetation Crust had brought earlier to be used as medication. Crust himself was pushing at the rear.

'I had enough with the piece you brought before,' Marsha informed them.

'This is for us,' Crust said, 'there's nuffink t' drink 'ere, 'cept this.'

'Drink?' Marsha asked, amazed.

'Taste it,' Packo invited him.

'But only suck,' Crust warned, 'eat it an' you'll be as sick as a parrot.'

'A what?' Marsha asked.

'Never mind,' Crust said smiling, 'just swaller the moisture an' spit out the pulp.'

Marsha did so. He took a bite and sat chewing. It was very refreshing. He spat the chunk out. 'Very good,' he commended

Crust. 'What is it?'

'The inside of the spiky plant,' Packo told him.

'Really! But how did you manage to slice this piece off?'

'Crust's an expert with a rock. He can curl his forepaw around one and throw it. With great accuracy, too, I might add.'

'That's interesting,' Marsha nodded, 'that's how you disposed of the eagle, by throwing a rock?'

'Yeah, one of me bettah shots that was. It was somefink I picked up at the dump.'

'The dump?' Marsha was beginning to wonder whether he would ever be able to have a conversation with Crust.

'Yeah, yer know, a rubbish tip.'

'I'm still not with you,' Marsha said honestly, 'what's a rubbish tip?'

'Obvious innit?' Crust answered. 'I mean, it's a place where the 'eaders put all their rubbish, yer know, all the stuff they want t' frow out.'

''Eaders?' Marsha asked.

'Yeah, yer know, the lanky lads wiv two legs.'

'Oh, you mean headers.'

'Yeah, that's wot I said, 'eaders.'

Now Marsha really was stunned. 'You lived near the 'eaders?'

'Yeah,' Crust smiled, 'Listen, you chew away there, and you too, Packo. I'll try t' explain about meself. Yer know, yer the first 'ares I've seen for ages. Yer gonna 'ave to tell me wot yer doin' 'ere. I mean, yer obviously don't live 'ere else you wouldn't be nearly starvin' t' death.'

'Right then,' Marsha agreed, 'we'll chew, you talk. After that we'll fill you in on ourselves.'

It was an amicable arrangement. 'Right,' Crust said, 'but first, is the big lad OK?'

'Sleeping,' Marsha replied, 'we'll keep him some food,'

'No need, sunshine, there's plenty out there,' Crust threw his head in the general direction of the exit. So he began his story.

He told them that he had been born at the rubbish tip. That's where he had learned to survive, 'eat anyfink as long as it don't make yer sick.' Life at the tip was not easy. Flocks of seagulls would descend to scavenge through the rubbish. To frighten them off Crust learned to throw anything that came to hand. He had a great friend, Jacko, 'me best mate.' Jacko was killed by a fox and Crust decided it was time to leave.

When he left the tip he found himself 'slap bang in the middle of the 'eaders land.' He'd had a torrid time, chased by dogs and nearly run over by cars. One evening he found a shed which was raised off the ground. He hopped inside and fell asleep. When he awoke he was on a 'trundler, yer know, them fings wot travel on the shiny tracks.' Marsha and Packo had no idea what he was talking about but they remained silent.

The train took him out of man's urban world and into open countryside. Twenty-four hours passed before he was presented with an opportunity to alight. The train slowed as it climbed a long steep hill. Crust jumped out and headed into the wilderness.

Marsh broke into Crust's account. 'How long ago was that?' he asked.

'Five nights, mate.'

'And how long have you been here?'

'Free nights. That greasebag eagle 'ad me trapped. 'e spotted me an' 'ad me in mind for 'is dinner. Luckily enuff I found this place. 'E couldn't get in.

'I 'ad t' be careful whenever I went out. I was watchin' 'im this evenin'. 'e lost interest in me so I figured that someone else was in trouble. All I needed was one good shot at that bleeder. Well, I got it. 'E won't be causin' us any more bovver. Yer see, I s'pose we 'ad a right stoppin' 'im killin' us. We wasn't causing 'im any trouble.'

'Thank you once again for saving us,' Marsha broke in as soon as the opportunity presented itself. 'What is of interest to me is that we are only two nights' journey from the point where you jumped from the trundler.'

'Yeah, that's about it.'

'Perhaps it won't be too far after that to the end of this wilderness.'

'No idea, mate,' Crust readily admitted.

'We must travel east. Is that the direction you came?'

'Yeah, that'd be it.'

'Crust is to come with us.' It was Packo. The words issued from him with a sudden intensity. 'He must join the quest. He has an important role to play.'

''E alright?' Crust asked Marsha.

'Oh, fine, fine,' Marsha replied. 'Will you join us?'

'Wot's all this about a quest?'

'Our quest is to search for the Land of Deep Shadow. We don't know where we'll end up.' Marsha would fill in the background details later. If Packo said that Crust should join them, it was imperative that he agree.

'The Land of Deep Shadow. Sounds like a bit of an adventure.'

'You could say that,' Marsha replied.

'OK, sunshine. Count me in.'

Chapter Thirteen

Lotto had been fortunate. Packo's timely intervention had saved his life as surely as Lotto had saved him at the Chaos Chasm. Lotto slept all that day while the others snoozed and shuffled in the stifling heat. When he finally awoke Lotto was more than willing to continue with the journey. Marsha, however, decided against it. He reasoned that it would serve them better to hole up for another twenty-four hours. They needed the rest. Their newly found source of moisture from the cacti replenished them and should provide provision enough to cross the wilderness. Their meeting with Crust had been fortuitous, and possibly more. Packo's gift as Seer seemed to prove that it had been preordained; Marsha hoped that the old hare might appear and shed some light on their destination. He didn't.

The night was cool, pleasantly so after the heat of the day. Dawn broke once more and the sun climbed the sky. The oppressive heat returned. Crust kept them supplied with fresh cactus and they eagerly sucked its moisture into their bodies. When they weren't dozing Crust kept them amused. He was a gregarious character and made the most of their companionship. He took a particular liking to Lotto and was for ever asking him how he was. For their part, Marsha, Packo, and Lotto began to acclimatise to his strange dialect, learning to understand his meaning by following the context. Despite that they still had to stop him occasionally to enquire what exactly he was talking about. Thus the day was spent.

As night fell, Lotto announced that he was well enough to travel. Marsha was not convinced but Lotto stepped out from under the flat slab of rock and stretched. The blotches along his flanks showed a dim red where the blood had stained his fur.

'It's probably best for me to be moving,' he insisted, 'I'll only stiffen up if I remain still. Listen, I've had a great rest, and although I'm a bit sore, I'd prefer to move on. Let's try to put this wilderness behind us.'

'If you're quite sure,' Marsha said.

'I'm sure.'

That was that. A star strewn sky adorned the heavens, a million twinkling eyes laughing at them as they stole across the wilderness. A deathly silence held firm. Even the talkative Crust respected it and, for once, kept his thoughts to himself.

Dawn approached, grey on the eastern horizon. Then the giant red ball rose above the ground and began to flood the dimly lit world with its light and heat. Dawn in the wilderness was a magnificent sight. The huge bloodied orb emerged slowly, majestically fanning light rays over the ground and streaking the sky, driving the darkness away.

Marsha marvelled at the awesome sight. Nature never ceased to stun him. It impelled him beyond his own insignificant life to appreciate that someone was indeed responsible for all that was, including his own fragile existence. Yet, he remained ever the pragmatist. He admired the sunrise momentarily and then began to cast his eyes about for a safe form in which to spend the day. He was not alone in having such thoughts uppermost in his mind.

''Ere,' Crust shouted, 'this should do us.' He jerked his head towards a hollow in the shade of an overhanging rock.

Marsha nodded. It would serve them well.

'Might as well get us a bit t' chew,' Crust said. He ran towards the nearest cactus, sniffed and rejected it. He ran over to another. This one satisfied him. He searched the ground and on finding a medium sized rock took it in his right forepaw. He drew back and fired it with a strength which belied his stature. It flew fast and true, spliting the main green trunk. He selected another rock, took aim, and fired. It fractured the trunk two feet above the split and a huge chunk hung loose. He raced forward and tore it off. Triumphantly he dragged it back to the makeshift form.

'Very impressive,' Marsha told him, smiling.

'Fanks.' Crust removed a strip and passed it to Lotto. 'There yer are, mate, chew that.'

'That's very kind of you,' Lotto said. 'I've never seen anything like that before, the throwing I mean.'

'Fink nuffink of it. I'll teach yer. Look, yer take a rock in yer paw like this. Take a good grip an' keep yer eye on the target. Then . . .'

Marsha's ears pricked. Perhaps Crust might be able to help in one of his earlier concerns, teaching Lotto to fight. There was no time like the present.

'An' that's all there is to it,' Crust concluded.

'How are you feeling, Lotto?' Marsha asked.

'Well, thank you.'

'No, really,' Marsha insisted, 'how are the wounds?'

'I can still feel the odd twinge,' Lotto answered honestly, 'but they are getting better all the time.'

Marsha turned his attention to Crust. 'I suppose you've done a fair amount of fighting in your time, Crust?'

'Yeah, I s'pose I ave.'

'And tell me,' Marsha probed teasingly, 'what's the secret of being a good fighter? I take it you can handle yourself. You've had a tough life and you've survived.'

'Well, fanks for the confidence.' Crust enjoyed the praise. Packo and Lotto began to listen with increasing interest.

'There's no real secret. This is wot I fink, for wot it's worf. Never fight if yer can avoid it. I mean, don't go lookin' for a scrap. That's dumb. Yer can end up in lotsa bovver that way. 'Avin' said that, there are times yer can't avoid it. If that 'appens, try t' use the element of surprise, get the first blow in, an' make it 'urt. If yer lucky enuf to do that, scarper, get out of it if yer can.

Never gloat; 'angin' round is a dead alley.'

'What if you were fighting, say, someone the size of Lotto,' Marsha asked, innocently, 'where would you hit him?'

I'd go for the eyes. I'd try t' blind im for a moment so I could eiver smack 'im 'ard on the snout, or, better still, get a good kick into 'is breavers.'

'Breavers?' Packo asked.

'Yeah, yer know, ere.' Crust pointed to his own rib cage. 'Above all, I'd do me best not t' be 'it by 'im. 'E's a big lad an' should pack quite a clout.'

'I've never had a proper fight in my life,' Lotto said. 'Marsha and Packo will tell you about the first time I met them. I thought that my sheer physical size would make them whimper. It didn't. It was the beginning of the turning point in my life. I was such a bully, a coward. I'm ashamed to think of it now.' Lotto fell silent, brooding over his past indiscretions.

'Yer've never 'ad a scrap!' Crust said, astonished.

'Really, Crust, it's true, I wouldn't know how to hit you.'

'Prove it, 'it me.' He held his head forward inviting a blow. 'Just try. Believe me, yea won't 'urt me, I've bin around.'

Lotto was unsure.

Marsha was pleased. Everything was working out to his satisfaction. He winked at Packo, conveying to him that he should allow the situation to develop.

'Cam on my son, give me a slug.'

'If you're really certain,' Lotto finally agreed reluctantly.

'Yeah, yeah,' Crust pointed to his chin. 'ard as yer can.' Lotto swung out delivering an unmerciful blow. Crust avoided the worst of it by carrying through with the punch. However, it still stung him.

'Blaw-dy 'ell! I fought yer couldn't 'it!'

'I'm most dreadfully sorry, Crust,' Lotto began to apologise profusely, 'I didn't realise, I'm . . .'

'Leave it out, Lotto,' Crust interrupted him. 'OK, I felt it, but I moved wiv it, didn't I? It was not as bad as it might 'ave bin. I'll tell yer wot, yer a natural. 'Ere, 'ave anover go.'

'Are you sure?'

'Yeah, ride on, my son.'

Lotto delivered another blow, this time with his left paw, and this time it did take Crust by surprise. It knocked him out cold! He lay spread-eagled. It was several moments before he began to come to.

'Stone the crows,' he groaned, 'yer can't 'alf deliver em.' Lotto was mortified. He began to apologise all over again. 'I'm very sorry . . .'

Crust struggled to his feet. 'Naw,' he said, waving his paw to silence Lotto, 'we know that yer can 'it, and with either paw too. Good, I'm gonna presume yer can kick wiv yer 'ind legs, never met a 'are wot couldn't. Anyway, I'm not gonna invite yer t' prove it t' me. When yer in a scrap yer 'alf way there if yer can deliver a blow. There's somefink else equally important. Yer've gotta learn t' parry blows an' t' go wiv the flow when yer do get 'it. I'll show yer.' Marsha and Packo sat back, the street kid teaching the reformed bully. Fascinating.

'Naw, if I 'it yer like this,' Crust struck a short jab carrying no weight directly to Lotto's snout, 'wot yer gonna do?' Lotto stared back blankly.

'OK. Let's start wiv somefink simple. If I 'it yer wiv me right, yer move yer' ead t' yer right. If I 'it yer wiv me left, yer move yer ead t' yer left. Simple innit? Let's practise that. Just remember, go wiv it, go wiv it.' Crust dealt Lotto gentle blows and Lotto found that he instinctively moved with them.

'Remember, Lotto, always move the direction the blow is goin'. Course, yer ave t' watch out. If I'm on yer right, itting yer wiv me right, then yer go left. Go wiv the blow. Got it?'

'I believe I have,' Lotto grinned enormously.

'Naw, if yer can take the sting outta the blow, so can yer opponent. If 'e's a fighter, 'e'll know the tricks too. Wot yer've gotta do is outwit 'im. For example, make t' 'it 'im wiv yer right, and smack 'im with yer left instead. If yer can do that 'e's duckin' into yer punch. Let's try it.'

Crust showed the way, leading with his right, then, quick as a flash, springing his left paw. He made Lotto practise that and then the reverse tactic, leading left, punching right.

'Good, innit?' Crust laughed, 'yer learnin' fast. Naw, the one I mentioned at the beginnin', the front jab. Idea is t' land a blow smack on the snout. Very effective it can be, 'urts like 'ell too. If someone tries that yer must put yer paws up, block it. 'Ere, try it.' Lotto jabbed, Crust blocked. Then Lotto defended himself. 'Very good,' Crust enthused, 'see, there's nofink to it.'

Lotto was about to answer when a strange noise sounded from the darkness beneath the nearby rock. Everyone froze. Then, as if a ripple of static electricity passed through them, they stood aghast. A snake slithered slowly and purposefully into view. Then they heard the noise again, a rattle, like shaken stones. It was nearest to Crust. This was something well outside his previous experience and he was petrified. The fangs opened, issuing a hiss. This was followed by the rattle, chill, menacing, hypnotic. The atmosphere was charged. Crust, shocked and terrified, was to be the target. The snake's poison would leave him dead within moments. The snake sprang, spitting vehemently. Its slit eyes poured hatred, its fangs, huge and gaping, breathed poison.

It was the thud that made Crust jump. At precisely the time the snake struck, the rock caught him, splitting the evil head.

'Ahaaa. I did it, I did it, Crust I did it.' It was Packo. 'Remember, you showed me how to throw rocks at the spiky plants.' Crust was still in a daze.

'Well, I threw the rock just like you showed me and I got him.' Packo was delighted with himself.

'Cor, fanks.'

Lotto moved forward. 'Are you all right, Crust?'

'Yeah mate, I'm alright.'

Lotto spoke gently to him. 'You've been teaching me, Crust, perhaps I can teach you something, or at least advise you.' Crust gazed at him blankly.

'You see, Crust, you were surprised, shocked. As a result your mind ceased to function. You've always got to react, not necessarily physically, always mentally. We're going into the unknown; never be comfortable, never.'

'I'll do me best t' remember that, Lotto, fanks.'

Marsha was surprised. Here was another side to Lotto's character. The former extrovert bully who couldn't fight, who was once so loud and aggressive, had become quiet and unassuming, able to endure pain and suffering, and now he was beginning to show the depth of his character. His experience of accepting himself and putting others first was producing a nobility long since smothered by a brash exterior.

The sun was by now a blazing, blinding yellow. They tried to relax in the shade of the rock. The day passed slowly. Chewing cactus was keeping them alive, affording them the minimal amount of moisture and protein to keep absolute dehydration and hunger at bay. Yet, it was abundantly clear that they were far from their fittest. Thirst and hunger were constant, nagging companions.

They travelled on that night. Mountains came into view in the distance and edged closer as the night turned to dawn. Crust suddenly became very excited.

'Down there, down there,' he shouted. He pointed to a small cluster of trees and bushes, green against the barrenness.

'Bit a grub down there, yer can bet yer 'ind legs on it. Cam on.'

Crust waited no longer. He scurried down the stony slope. Caught up in his enthusiasm the rest followed. A decent meal would indeed be welcome. Marsha did not recognise the trees. He looked at them closely, finally finding what he sought. Hidden amongst the leaves were small clusters of unripened nuts, light brown in colour and still protected by green outer leaves. He pulled a few off with his teeth.

'Search for these,' he advised. 'We can crack them open, they'll be safe to eat.' They searched frantically. In a short while they had built up a surprisingly large collection. They stripped the outer leaves and began cracking the nuts with their teeth.

Lotto was also munching, the nuts were good. His eyes were

darting around, surveying the small area supporting the rogue trees. It was strange that they had grown here. He noticed a green patch of ground and hopped over to it. He sniffed and pressed his snout against it. Then he clawed the ground and pulled the weed up revealing a stony, slightly moist soil. He jumped over it and began pushing the earth out with his hind paws. He showered the others with stones and fine, coarse earth.

'Wot the 'eck! ' Crust shook the earth from his coat. Lotto was already five inches down and the ground was becoming moister. Packo trotted over and opened a new hole alongside Lotto's.

Marsha smiled. 'Why didn't I think of that?' he murmured, 'I must be getting old.'

'Fink of wot?' Crust asked increduously.

'It's here, it's here,' Lotto shouted.

The two holes joined and suddenly water appeared, brown at first and then clearing as the underground current surfaced.

Lotto took a huge gulp. 'Hey, it's cool and fresh and . . .' He dipped in again taking several large mouthfuls. Packo was already gulping when Crust arrived, leaping in amongst them, showering them all with the contents of the continuously filling hole. He splashed and laughed, drank, splashed, and laughed again.

Marsha idled over and put his mouth to the source of the bubbling spring. The cold soothed and washed his throat, swilling the dry grittiness away. He couldn't help but smile and wonder. It was obvious that there must be some sort of water supply here, trapped beneath the surface, hence the trees. Now Lotto had become a water diviner, whatever next? As he felt the water revive him he blessed Lotto for his astuteness in bringing it to the surface. They found more nuts and ate them, then drank more from the still gurgling spring. The simple fare was sheer luxury. Suddenly, far off in the distance, they heard the sound. Crust rushed to the outermost tree and gazed into the valley.

'A smokah, a smokah,' he shouted, 'diff'rent t' the one I 'ad a lift on, but it's a trundler all the same, believe me.'

Marsha, Packo, and Lotto sprang forward and followed Crust's gaze down into the valley. It was like a snake crawling along, puffing smoke from its head. It was just beginning to ascend the long, steep climb to the ridge which was perhaps a mile ahead of them.

'It musta bin up there I jumped off, I could 'ave run faster than it was travellin'.' Crust jerked his head to the left and there, streaking up the mountain side, caught in the rays of the sun was a strange, long, white hot glow.

'That's 'em, the 'ard tracks wot keep the trundler on course.'

'So, my friends, you've almost achieved the final leg of your journey.'

The hares spun round. The Purveyor stood before them. They stared at him, shocked. How did he always manage to be ahead of them?

'I prepared this area a very long time ago. It is good that you have made such use of it to replenish you after the bitterness of the wilderness. Towards the back of the trundler you'll find a truck with an opening. You must jump on. Crust will advise you. The trundler is travelling north, that is the direction you must now take. I shall advise you when your journey is over.'

'But . . .' Marsha was struggling to speak.

'Go to the high point, go now. Do not miss this opportunity.' The Purveyor turned and hopped from the shelter of the small trees and disappeared behind a cluster of rocks.

''Ere, where's e gone?' Crust stepped forward to investigate.

'There's no point,' Marsha told him, 'you won't find him.'

'We've got to get on that trundler,' Packo said. 'Yeah,' Crust replied. 'If we go t' a spot just below the highest point we'll be able t' jump on 'andy enuff. Cam on.'

Crust shot off, taking charge of the situation. He knew all about trundlers and he would shoulder the responsibilty. He followed a route roughly parallel to the tracks, glancing continually to his right and adjusting his course when the need arose. They were climbing towards the butt end of the valley. When he considered that they had achieved sufficient height he turned towards the tracks. The hares were very nearly at the northernmost tip of the glacial shed. The track began a long curve, winding its metal way through the mountains.

'This will do us,' Crust said. 'The trundler's comin'.'

They gazed down the track. The train was no more than a hundred paces away. The great iron beast belched black smoke as it strained under the burden of having to haul its long and heavy load up the ever steepening mountain.

'Crouch an' wait,' Crust ordered, 'I'll tell yer when.'

The monster was bearing down on them, puffing and hissing. The ground began to shudder and the air was a cacophony of violent noise. Marsha, Packo, and Lotto automatically cowered as the great black devil drew alongside them. Steam hissed from the huge body of the beast as it cried out in its misery, labouring to drag its tremendous burden on and up. Crust smiled and savoured again the oh so familiar odour, the oily smoky pall that clings to a great steam engine.

The stock began to roll past, their couplings knocking, shunting, rattling, music to Crust's ears. The others dared hardly look, the tremendous din deafening them, threatening.

'There, there!' Crust shouted above the mayhem. 'The truck wiv the openin'. That's the one for us, cam on, shift it.' He urged them to life. Taking the lead he bounded forward and leapt aboard.

'Cam on, cam on,' Crust shouted from the opening, cajoling them to join him.

Packo took careful aim at the opening and jumped. He landed with a thud on the hard, metallic floor. Marsha did likewise. Lotto gazed, panic etched across his face.

'Cam on, Lotto, cam on me ole mate.'

Lotto jumped. He was so terrified that he lost his footing and managed only to attain the lip of the opening. The hares watched in horror as he slipped under the truck and disappeared from view.

The dark undercarriage of the train swallowed him.

Chapter Fourteen

'Blaw-dy 'ell,' Crust shouted. ''E's bin run over!' He peered over the side of the truck, staring back to the point on the track where Lotto had disappeared.

'I'm going to look for him,' Marsha said, 'to find out.'

'Nah,' Crust raised his paw, 'I'm used t' these fings, I'll go. There'll still be time to get back on.'

He jumped out and landed lightly on the rocky ground. He ran back, scouring the land. No sign of Lotto. The last of the trucks rolled past. Crust glanced at the rear of the final truck as if he expected to see Lotto sitting comfortably on the unused coupling, grinning at him. He wasn't. He looked down the track, and there, huddled and shaking, lay Lotto. He raced to him.

'Lotto,me ole mate, yer safe.'

Lotto breathed a sigh of relief. 'Crust, am I glad to see you. I fell under the truck and landed in between the hard tracks. I thought I was going to die.'

'No bovver t' yer. Yer 'urt at all?'

'No,' Lotto replied standing and shaking himself.

'We've gotta join the uvers. Will yer try again?'

'You're dead right I will,' Lotto said emphatically.

'Cam on then, when that trundler reaches the top of the valley it will begin to pick up speed. We've gotta be aboard by then.'

They hopped on to the side of the tracks and began to sprint. They reached the last truck and overtook it. One, two, three, four, how far was the opening? Five, six, and there it was. Marsha and

Packo were peering out, shouting to them, urging them on.

'Keep goin',' Crust commanded, 'we must get a'ead, then we'll be able t' stand back and take a run at it.'

The engine had now reached the top of the valley and was beginning to veer right as it entered the plateau between the mountains. The trucks to the rear were still dragging it back. Soon that would change and the train would gather momentum. Crust was aware of the situation. Time was running out. Already the lie of the land to the left of them was beginning to drop away. Their approach to the open truck would be up hill. And there was an an extra difficulty, the ground was shaley.

They were six trucks ahead. 'Quick,' Crust shouted, 'down ere.' He took seven paces down, lined Lotto up, and took up his own position immediately behind him. 'This is it, Lotto mate. When I say go, yer go. I'll be right be'ind yer. I'll tell yer when t' jump. Dig yer 'ind legs in and give it all yer've got. There's only one chance.'

Three trucks had passed already. Crust studied the situation carefully. Another truck passed, then another. They could see Marsha and Packo in the opening, looking out anxiously. Half of the sixth truck passed.

'Go for it,' Crust shouted.

Lotto sprang forward determined to cast his fear aside and make good. The opening yawned in front of him.

'Jump!' Crust shouted.

Lotto dug in, moved his body back in order to shift his weight on to his powerful hind legs, and jumped. He sailed over Marsha and Packo and landed in an untidy heap at the other side of the truck.

'I made it,' he shouted joyful as he picked himself up. 'Crust, I made it.' He turned round.

Marsha and Packo were staring out. Lotto sprang forward. 'Where is he?' he demanded, 'Where's Crust?' He looked out. Crust was tumbling down the escarpment, rolling over and over on the steep, rough ground.

'Crust, Crust,' Lotto shouted. He made to shoulder past

Marsha and Packo, intending to jump to Crust's assistance as Crust had done for him.

Marsha restrained him. 'It's no use, Lotto,' he said firmly and quietly. 'The trundler is picking up speed. There is no chance of Crust getting aboard now.'

'He must, he must,' Lotto was beside himself. 'It's all my fault, all my fault.'

'No,' Packo tried to calm him. 'Crust lost his footing on the loose rocks.'

The truck began to veer away. They gazed out. Crust's precipitous fall had come to a halt by a huge boulder. His body lay still. It was their last sight of him.

The train picked up speed. Their ears were filled with disconnected sound, the sh-de-sh of the motion of the trucks and their passage over the rails. The scenery flew past. The experience would have been exhilarating but for the loss of Crust. He had come into their lives briefly, yet they all grieved his passing.

Lotto was inconsolable. He blamed himself entirely for the whole, disastrous episode. Eventually he fell into a fitful sleep, the involuntary movements of his body attesting to his agitated state of mind. Marsha and Packo found the release of sleep hard to come by. They were as upset as Lotto by Crust's loss and understood his depression. It was a fretful day. Occasionally the train would stop and there would be great commotion around the engine. The hares lay low until they once more started to be carried along faster than they had ever travelled in their lives. The motion of the train, strange and reverberating, prevented them from sleeping except in snatches. The train hurtled through the mountains. On occasions total darkness enveloped them. They opened their eyes wide, frightened by the terrifying experience, wondering what could be happening. Then, suddenly, they would break out into light again. They could only wonder what had caused the sudden transformation from day to night and back again.

Eventually they became accustomed to the train's motion. When it stopped to take on water they hopped off and fed. Lotto began to come round and to accept that Crust's premature departure was not his fault. He had become very fond of the little fellow and he would not forget him or the lessons he had learned about how to fight.

The hares awoke to begin their fourth day on the train. The end of the truck, downwind from the opening, was sprinkled white. They had been transported into a winter landscape. Packo leapt towards the opening. He had never been to this place before, yet it held a strange and sinister hold over him.

'I do believe we're almost there,' he said to Marsha and Lotto.

'Very nearly but not quite.' Packo spun round. The Purveyor's kindly eyes burned into his.

'Where are we going?' Packo asked, his question cutting to the core.

'To the Land of Deep Shadow,' the Purveyor replied.

'What will we find there?'

'Hell itself.'

'What must we do?'

'Confront the evil.'

Packo fell silent. He was asking questions but receiving answers that he did not understand.

All three hares fixed their eyes upon the Purveyor. He had disappeared too often in the past. Now, they held him with their stare. He was trapped.

'You must travel across the mountain.' The Purveyor yanked his head, indicating a point somewhere beyond the opening. Not one of the hares dared look.

'Come, come,' the old hare chuckled, 'believe me, I can disappear at will, whether you are staring at me or not. So please, don't be afraid to look.' Packo turned, the only one to do so, as if he sensed the truth of the words. Away on the horizon a white, rounded mountain stood out, sentinel to the range beyond.

'On the other side of that your task really begins.'

'And what is that task?' Marsha asked.

'To bring light to the gloom, to remove the shadow.'

'Tell us directly,' Marsha ordered, tiring of the cryptic answers.

'That which is hidden will be revealed soon enough. The trundler will stop not an hour from now. That will be your sign to alight. What lies ahead of you and its outcome is not preordained. You must use your wits, your talents, your powers of endurance. Go, knowing that only you are capable of fulfilling the task. Take nothing for granted.' Then, to their utter amazement, the Purveyor simply vanished.

'Now I've seen everything,' Lotto said.

'Or seen nothing!' Marsha joked. 'Well, not long now, let's sit tight and wait.'

They sat at the truck's opening, watching and waiting. They were oblivious to the rushing cold. The eager anticipation of the end of their marathon journey, rather than the icy blast, numbed them. The ground beneath them continued to be swallowed up as the train bore on and on. The mountain the Purveyor mentioned loomed large. It was rounded, its summit a conical shape. This was covered with a thin layer of snow. A late afternoon sun broke through, lifting their spirits. Each hare was lost to his own thoughts. The journey had been long and arduous. They had almost arrived, yet they still did not know what to expect, what they would find. Marsha's thoughts returned to the savaged hare; that had been the beginning. He did not bother to ask himself how that hare had made the long, wearisome journey. That did not seem to matter too much. But he did ask himself, yet again, what it was all supposed to mean.

Packo's thoughts were also centred on the past. His journey had begun with the cruel death of his sister, Dersall. That arbitrary killing had catapulted him this far. Whatever it was he was destined to do, it would soon be revealed.

Lotto stared at the fleeing landscape. He recalled his past life, the shame and the ignominy. This was his chance to make reparation for all that. He sat determined. Whatever his role, he was ready to embrace it.

Then there was a massive shudder. The noise reverberated

through the truck. The hares, experienced train travellers now, recognised immediately what was happening. The massive length of the train was grinding to a halt. They waited and watched and listened. The couplings clashed, grating together one moment, apart and taut the next. The land rolled by at a leisurely pace. The temptation was to jump, to be gone in search of their ultimate challenge. They sat still. They stole these last few moments of relative comfort and security, like one delaying his mandatory turn into the wind. The train ground to a halt. A whistle pierced the sudden silence.

'Well lads,' Marsha said, 'this is it. Ready?' Packo and Lotto nodded: their expressions were resolute, their eyes already focused on the conical mountain. Marsha hopped from the train. Packo and Lotto joined him. Their paws crunched through the thin, frozen layer of snow. It was little more than a quarter of an inch deep. It was good to feel the ground beneath their paws again. They sprang forward, a light, cool breeze freshening their snouts.

Ahead lay their destination, hidden still by the frozen mountain. They pressed onwards.

'. . . to confront the unknown is to confront the ultimate terror. When you enter that realm take with you all the experience life has taught you; know your strengths and weaknesses. Know too that fear can be overcome, for it is nothing more than a seeking after self. Put self behind you and your fear, however real, will fade. Those who have been called to follow these words will come, at last, to the final test. Embrace it . . .'

Prophecy of Tuarug 8 : 3-4

PART THREE: The Terror

Chapter Fifteen

The three hares travelled around the base of the first mountain. The snow was patchy. Coarse grass and bare heather lay exposed. Their journey took them in a huge semi-circle before they were able to gaze out on to the land beyond the mountain, a vast area punctuated by conical hills. It was dusk and all was tranquil.

As darkness fell they found a hollow comfortably closed in by heather. They sat huddled together, sharing their body heat. The silence was absolute. Yet it was not simply the silence that disturbed them. They would quickly adjust to that after the constant noise of the train. Silence to a hare is a close and treasured friend. There was something else, and it was Packo who voiced their shared anxiety.

'There is evil here,' he whispered. 'I can feel it, very near, hidden, lurking. This peaceful landscape is not what it appears.'

'One of us should keep watch,' Marsha suggested. 'You two catch some sleep. I'll wake you, Packo, later. Lotto, you can take the last stint. OK?'

They nodded. Lotto relaxed immediately and was very soon lost to the world. Packo found that he could not escape so easily. He sat still, trance-like, never blinking. Marsha constantly surveyed the scene. He did not intrude on Packo's thoughts. He simply watched.

A pale moon rose shedding an opaque light. The land lay bare before them. Nothing stirred. It was a cold night. It did not snow but a frost glistened as it formed.

'Packo,' Marsha whispered when he considered that approximately a third of the night had passed, 'Will you take the watch?'

'Yes,' Packo replied, 'You get some sleep.'

'You haven't slept at all have you, Packo?'

'Later perhaps, now it is time for me to be awake.'

There was a distance in Packo's voice. Marsha didn't pass any remarks. He snuggled against Lotto's bulky body and closed his eyes.

It seemed only moments later that he felt the sharp dig in his ribs.

'Marsha, Marsha, wake up.' Packo's voice was urgent. Marsha responded immediately.

'Out there,' Packo pointed directly ahead. 'On the level ground before the next mountain.'

Marsha focused his eyes and stared hard. 'Two creatures,' he said.

'Yes,' Packo confirmed, 'One is a hare, the other, I'm not sure.'

'Look, they're changing direction,' Marsha said, studying the situation. 'They are coming towards us. The one behind is smaller than the hare. Whatever it is, it's giving that poor hare a dreadful time, kicking and pushing and biting him. Packo, wake Lotto.'

The wretched hare moved slowly as it attempted to hop on three legs. One of his forepaws was tucked protectively under his body. He was scrawny and stumbled often. He seemed to be having difficulty seeing where he was going. The creature behind shoved and punched him causing the hare to cry out in anguish.

Captive and captor approached ever nearer. Marsha, Packo, and Lotto watched the sorry scene, a terrible realisation dawning on them. The bullying captor was also a hare! Strange looking to be sure, but most definitely a hare. He was entirely white and, as they had observed earlier, slightly smaller than the pitiful creature he goaded.

They lay perfectly still, blending with the dark brown woody shoots of the heather. The suffering hare was no more than ten paces away when Marsha and Packo charged. 'Hey,' Marsha shouted, 'leave him alone.' The brown hare halted and fell to the ground, frightened. The white hare, shocked at first, recovered his composure and stood arrogantly. Marsha and Packo thundered into him striking blows to his snout and flanks. He turned quickly and hobbled away.

Lotto's role had been to remain hidden, ready to confront any unforeseen danger. As soon as he was able to see the brown hare clearly he had forgotten the need to remain hidden. As Marsha and Packo turned their attention to the injured hare they found Lotto already there. He was standing over the brown, looking aghast at the shaking shivering hare before him, observing the ribs that protruded from the taut flesh along his flanks, wondering about the fur and why it was so blotched and dull.

'Please, please,' the brown pleaded, 'I'll go back. Please, please, no more.'

Lotto bent very close to the intimidated hare. 'Little one, you have nothing to fear. We're friends. It's all over now.' He pressed his body against the trembling frame of the brown, attempting to pass on his warmth and strength. Gently he passed his right forepaw over the head and flattened ears of the terrified hare while continuing to speak softly. 'We are your friends, you're safe now, stay with us, we'll protect you.'

The fragile brown took comfort and looked up at the kindly giant. Lotto saw his eyes, glazed, vacant, unseeing. The brown's head dropped then and his body relaxed. The slender thread of life to which he had clung had snapped. In his final moments of life he had found warmth and affection.

'Come,' Marsha said softly, 'let us place his body in the form we made for ourselves. Now, at least, he's free from the terror he must have suffered.'

Lotto bent and pushed his head under the hare's stomach allowing it to rest across his neck. He lifted it easily and carried it, drapped over him, to the heather sanctuary. He laid it to rest while Marsha and Packo broke the heather shoots over it, protecting it from the worst of the elements.

'Now to get some answers,' Marsha announced. 'That white hare hobbled out of here, he can't have got far. Let's go.'

They picked up the trail and began their pursuit. Paramount in their minds was indignation at the suffering and death they had witnessed. The landscape was eerie. Behind them the huge conical summit of the mountain, their guide to this strange land, pressed against the sky. Ahead smaller replicas dotted the terrain.

Marsha honed all his natural instincts in tracking the trail. He followed exactly the minute indentations in the frost-bound land. Then he picked up the smell of blood. The thought crossed his mind that this was odd. They had not inflicted an open wound on the hare. The indentations became heavier. The hare was struggling, they were closing in. Despite all his vigilance and expertise, Marsha nearly stepped on the body. It lay, naturally camouflaged, amongst the glistening frost. The white hare was dead, not as a result of their earlier attack upon him, but because of a savage beating he had received.

A scream pierced the silence. Suddenly, from the cover of the surrounding heather, four hares shot forward, forming a circle around Marsha, Packo and Lotto. The two groups stared at each other. The dead white lay in the centre. The three browns stared out, not at the strange pale breed they expected, but at four browns. No words were spoken. The silence held the challenge. To break the silence was to lay down the gauntlet. Marsha realised that to fight would serve no purpose. These browns were not the enemy.

'We have just discovered a hare,' he said quietly, with determination, 'a brown, one of our own, badly beaten. He died as a result of his injuries. If you inflicted those injuries then you are about to suffer his fate.'

The four hares twitched their snouts. They appeared anxious and unsure. No one moved; the confrontation did not relax.

Then, from somewhere beyond, a cry was raised. A group of whites emerged, strong, powerful protagonists. The four browns immediately cowered as the whites surrounded them. Marsha sized up the situation. He rotated his eyes to take in the entire circumference of the new circle. There were ten of them. Now he recognised the enemy.

'Packo, Lotto, let's get this done.'

The war was beginning and Crust's words echoed in their minds, 'Get in the first blow, 'urt em, don't gloat'. They charged out, their audacity taking the swanking whites by surprise. Lotto flew at one hitting him with an unmerciful blow to the snout, delivered a resounding thud into the flanks of another with a hind leg and smacked a third across the head with such force that his body left the ground. Marsha and Packo were just as effective, setting upon the arrogant whites with a vengeance. It was over in seconds. Five lay unconscious, three hobbled out of sight, and two had fled.

The four browns looked on, mystified. It was then that their leader reacted. 'We must leave here,' he said, 'come with us, quickly.'

Marsha, Packo and Lotto complied immediately. They travelled towards one of the smaller hills and, upon arriving, began to climb. It was deceptively steep. Despite this Marsha wondered why they were travelling so slowly. And there was something else. The browns did not look where they were going! They relied entirely on scent, following a set trail. Marsha could only wonder.

They were approximately a quarter of the way up when the leader of the browns stopped. There was a moment's hesitation before he broke left and began to search for something. 'Here,' he called. The other three immediately joined him and disappeared. Marsha, Packo and Lotto followed. They travelled down a tunnel until they arrived in a large chamber. From this five other tunnels led off into different parts of the mountain. This was to be the meeting place. The four hares sat. Marsha, Packo and Lotto settled down opposite them. They were a scrawny foursome. They were breathing heavily and their exhaled breath was very hoarse. Clearly, none of them was able to speak.

Marsha decided to take the initative.

'We have travelled a great distance,' he began. 'During our journey we were guided by a Purveyor. He told us that there is something we must accomplish here. We do not know what it is. Tonight we discovered a white hare bullying a brown. We drove the white off, but unfortunately the brown died. We went in search of the white in order to force some answers out of him. We found him dead. Then you arrived, followed closely by that group of whites. What's going on?'

Throughout, the four hares sat, their heads lowered, allowing their breathing to return to normal. As Marsha waited for an answer they looked up. Marsha saw them close to for the first time. Their eyes were glazed and vacant. They were like creatures without souls. The leading hare hesitated before he spoke, as if he was uncertain whether these strangers would understand what he was about to say.

'Is there a Seer among you?' he asked.

'I believe I am he,' Packo replied.

'Tell us then, what do you see?'

Packo could only answer honestly. 'Nothing out of the ordinary at this time. When my visions come and I speak, something happens to me. I cannot perform at will. I have no vision now. I see only what we all see.'

'Good, good,' the leader answered, pleased with the reply. His breathing was easier now, his voice gravelly and weak. 'That is the answer I would expect from a Seer. I apologise if we have appeared rude. We are very wary of any newcomers. I will tell you about ourselves.'

He paused to collect his thoughts. An ominous rattle in his throat accompanied his intake of breath as he readied himself to begin.

'We browns have lived here for many generations. Our mothers, in those intimate moments of new life, have impressed this upon us lest we ever forget or cease to realise. It is their duty to do so, a duty performed with the utmost loyalty. We are told, at the outset, that life was not always the deep shadow it has been for so very, very, long. Ours is a harsh land. When the snows come, and you have arrived just as they are about to begin in earnest, they stay with us for a third of the year. Our ancestors learned to cope with the elements, to respect the severe realities of their lives and live within their means.

'You see, they did this because this land, our land, was once so full of beauty. Isolated and free, they made their home here. It was safe, and, once they adapted to it, they discovered a rich and alluring land. The heather blooms in early summer and purple mountains sprout from the winter's white. As the blooms die off so the mountains take on a lovely brown-red hue which the sun caresses, creating such variegated colour that one can only sit and marvel. In the valleys bog cotton springs forth providing tender, succulent shoots whose white fluffy heads bob in the breeze. Mountain springs gush water so fresh and clear and pure. Food can be gathered then and taken back to the tunnels which provide shelter against the frozen cold of this time of year.

'We only know of such things because of our mothers who tell us of those halcyon days.' He paused then as he rekindled the memories.

'Then the whites came.' He struck up again, suddenly, as if there had been no pause. 'At first they came in ones and twos. We — I mean our ancestors — were suspicious of them. We were suspicious simply because they were different. It soon became more than that. They were haughty, patronising. They treated us like underlings. Apart from their colouring, their slightly smaller build, and their manner, the whites were much the same as ourselves. We came to accept their periodic visitations. Little did we know! They infiltrated our community, came to know our ways, shared our lives, and eventually enjoyed our friendship. We accepted them. They were very clever too. They recognised that we resented their patronising, so they stopped. They pretended to treat us as equals. We were innocent.

'The mountains are riddled with tunnels. How they were dug out, no one knows. We explored them and discovered their secrets. Those which are situated deep inside the mountain were seldom used. The ones nearer to the surface suited our needs and we tended to live only in them. They sheltered us in winter and provided a dry place to store food. The whites were fascinated with the tunnels and probed all the arterial routes in this mountain. It all seemed innocent enough.

'After several visits, several explorations, the whites disappeared. A whole summer passed and there was no sign of them. Then, about this time of year, as the first snows fell, they returned. A force of about twenty attacked from the open ground to the north, a similar number came through the tunnels to the south. They had done their homework. We are not a fighting group, we shrank before them, captured before we knew what was happening. They set us to work, digging. Some of the does were removed to tend the leverets. Once the leverets were considered able-bodied they were put to work too. Each doe was instructed to have a minimum of one litter a year. Any who failed were unmercifully killed, savaged by a group of whites who specialise in such atrocities. After three such killings the bucks agreed to co-operate. So, the workforce is continually renewing itself. Any who become old or infirm and cannot work, the whites' terror squad mutilate and leave to die in the Cavern of Bones.

'We have lived here as slaves for many generations. We are powerless to break free, our fate is sealed. We four are a small group who escaped. We attempt to pick off whites but we meet with little success and they will catch us soon, now that winter is coming. The terror squad you confronted tonight were searching for us. They'll be back.'

He fell silent as if everything had been explained.

'Why will they find it easy to catch you?' Marsha asked. 'Surely you know the territory now as well as they. A small group such as yourselves could be a real thorn in their sides. Your exploits could give hope to those still held in slavery.'

'We are virtually blind when out in the snow, the light is too much for us. We were born underground and never allowed into the open. The result is that our eyes are useless to us above ground when it is light. Below ground we can see a little but the whites gritted us, it is their policy.'

'What do you mean by gritted?' Packo asked.

'They hold the leverets' eyes open and kick tiny sharp stones in that scratch the surface. Not only does it impair our vision but it also makes us move around with our eyes half closed. We are never allowed water to wash them out and often the grit remains for many days. The whites repeat this at regular intervals. We've been washing our eyes out regularly and can now open them, but we cannot bear the light. We venture out at night but even the moon's opaque light is painful. Once the snows come we'll have real problems.'

'Do you mind if I see your eyes?' Marsha asked. He moved towards the leader and studied the open eyes. The pupils were badly scratched and there was still some grit lodged under the lids. 'We should be able to help you clean those out properly,' he said, 'at least you would not have any pain then. What is your name?'

'Para,' he replied, 'and this is Snappo, Tamol, and Turna.' He pointed to each of his three companions.

'I'm Marsha, this is Packo, that's Lotto.'

'Para,' Packo said, 'you mentioned before that the whites make you dig. What are you digging for?'

'Ice rocks!'

'And what are they?' Packo asked, still none the wiser.

'They are very hard rocks which glisten and shine. The whites value them as objects of worship. Whenever one is found they store it and eventually, when they have enough, they carry them away. Back to their own homes, I imagine.'

'The whites don't live here, then?' Marsha asked.

'Only one never leaves. He's their leader here, Swengli. He runs the entire operation. A real thug he is. He has personally killed more of our kind than the rest of the whites put together. He operates on the principle of fear, and very effective it is too. About every two months a new contingent of whites arrives, about thirty in all. The ones here disappear and return two months later. They take the rocks with them when they go. That seems to be how it works.'

'How many browns are there?' Marsha wanted all the facts.

'Fifty-three diggers, including us, and four does rearing leverets!'

'Now,' Marsha began. He got no further.

A group of whites flooded into the chamber from one of the tunnels.

'Swengli,' Para whispered. He had not expected the terror squad to hunt them here. Neither had he expected Swengli himself to lead them. That could mean only one thing: annihilation.

Chapter Sixteen

The chamber was filling with whites. Confrontation loomed. Swengli was flanked on either side by two hares. The others brought up the rear assembling like an arrowhead with the savage Swengli, a mocking leer etched across his face, the foremost tip. The browns, with Lotto nearest, stood silently and watched.

'For the first time the forces have met; but this is not the time to prove courage or to win the war.' Packo's voice trailed through the stillness and even Swengli stood rigid, caught in its strange intensity.

'Snappo, Tamol, Turna, left, meet base four. Marsha, Lotto, Packo, follow me.' Para's terse instructions broke the spell. Lotto scooped up a handful of gravel from the ground and flung it at the whites. They were stung into action. Swengli stood back as his flanking cover charged. The other browns were already leaving. The four whites charged at Lotto. He stood firm, planting a straight jab direct to the snout of the first which immediately drew blood and rendered him unconscious. The second jumped over him, hoping to take him from the rear while he was busy dealing with the third. Packo met the second as he landed, sending his head spinning with a forepaw blow. The third and fourth approached together. Marsha came forward, dodging a weak punch before his own struck home on top of the white's head. Lotto took care of the fourth by head butting his flanks, cracking ribs in the process.

Swengli stood back, his eyes were ablaze, the leer temporarily dropping from his mouth.

'Come,' Para shouted, 'leave them.'

Snappo, Tamol, and Turna were well away already.

'Let's get out of here,' Marsha called, 'we'll catch up with these later.' He had noticed that more whites were funnelling into the chamber. It would be folly to stay. They turned to leave.

'Ha! Cowards, not as brave as you think,' Swengli roared.

Packo faced him. 'Keep looking over your shoulder. You are going to pay for your crimes soon.'

Swengli, enraged by the taunt, rushed forward. Lotto deftly picked up the body of the white which was lying in front of him and hurled it at Swengli. He was sent crashing backwards. The brown hares disappeared and as he came to Swengli shouted his abuse into the tunnel down which they had fled.

'You'll beg me for mercy, and know this, there will be none, none.'

The words followed them, the threat they carried, the tone of the voice, the obvious hatred, the thirst for revenge; these were haunting. They had quite an enemy. Their paths would surely cross again.

The tunnel down which Para led them was criss-crossed by others every fifteen paces or so. He ignored them and plunged ever downwards in the very bowels of the earth. Then, suddenly, he turned left and then began a series of sharp directional changes, a ruse to create problems in the event of them being followed. Finally they came to an opening.

'Base four,' Para gasped as he tried frantically to catch his breath. From the periphery of the chamber Snappo, Tamol, and Turna came forward. They, too, were badly out of breath. Marsha, Packo, and Lotto had run hard but their breathing was unaffected. Several moments elapsed before the four began to show signs of recovery. During that time Marsha was constantly on guard against the possibility of an attack, 'Why didn't they follow us?' he asked.

'The whites don't know this area,' Para replied, his voice

hoarse. 'This is a safe place for us, the winding ways imbued into our minds since early days. The whites do not dig here and so, even if originally they might have explored the tunnels thoroughly, our present taskmasters have not bothered. If they attempted to follow us they would get lost. Get lost down here and you might never see the light of day again. This is why we are here now: Swengli will not lead the whites into the unknown.'

'Perhaps he is not as brave as he would like to imagine,' Lotto suggested.

'He is not foolish,' Para told him. 'Here we are no threat to him. He knows that if we want him, we'll eventually go to him. Then he'll be in territory he is familiar with. He has survived so long because he has the wisdom to know his weakness. Never underestimate him. And yet, in his wisdom, he has little knowledge. Heed this well. If you ever get lost in the underground labyrinth, follow one rule. Always take two rights, then a left. If you continue to do that it will lead you out, no matter where you are. The Ancients discovered that and even in digging new tunnels we have preserved that pattern unknown to the whites.'

'You were lucky that that information was not passed on to the whites when they first arrived,' Marsha said.

'No. That is sacred information, only passed to those who would show friendship by defending us. You have done that twice already. You deserve to know. It might save your lives one day.'

'Thank you, Para,' Marsha replied, 'but how can you be sure that we are friends?'

Para smiled. 'In all our history since our days of slavery began, we are taught that one day a Seer would come. When that day came we would recognise him, simply know. I know Packo to be so, although I don't know how or why. And now,' he shook himself, 'I will show you the hell you've come to. Then perhaps we can make plans.'

'Lead on,' Marsha said.

They travelled through another series of tunnels which

eventually led them out into the night air. It was very cold and the sky was heavy. Para and his companions were breathing raucously once again. They had not complained during the journey through the tunnels but now they were suffering. Para held his head low, the cold, bracing air stinging his lungs. Snappo and Tamol took up similar positions while Turna, obviously the runt of a litter, collapsed completely, his throat rattling with each intake of breath. Lotto approached him and stroked his strangely coarse hair with his forepaw. Neither Marsha, Packo, nor Lotto spoke. They recognised the suffering, silence seemed the apt response. Gradually some sort of normality returned.

'Tell us what ails you, Para?' Marsha probed gently.

'It's our lungs,' Para gasped. His voice was low and raking. 'You see, we have spent all of our lives underground. I mean all with the exception of the last month when we made a break for it. The digging we were forced to do creates dust which we inhale. It has left us like this. We can only run for short distances. That's why we spend most of our time stalking. We attack only when there is a good chance that we won't have to flee.'

'Now we must descend a little.' He led them down the mountain and into another concealed entrance where he turned to speak to them again. 'We shall need to be extremely cautious. I am going to show you the digging area. Snappo, Tamol, Turna, there is no need for you to accompany us. Go to level seven, our usual hiding place. We'll meet you there later.'

They departed silently.

'They don't say much, do they?' Lotto said.

'Snappo and Tamol are dumb, the result of punishment meted out by the whites. Swengli or one of his thugs ripped their tongues out when they were leverets. Such atrocities force the rest of us to comply. As for Turna, he's a shy fellow.'

Lotto was shocked. 'I . . . I had no idea.'

'That is why I must show you the diggings. Then you will know what life here is all about.'

He travelled slowly. They were climbing, the slope gradually becoming steeper. Para was suffering again but he gamely struggled on, on and up, weaving through tunnels. Finally they achieved a lofty perch overlooking an area of frenzied activity.

While Para slumped to the ground the others gazed into the abyss. Some forty paces below, the ground crawled with brown hares. They scurried back and forth pushing earth and rock with their forepaws. Most of the dirt was left behind. The rocks were stacked against one wall. Two whites sat and examined each one minutely. Four browns were attempting to smash the larger rocks with smaller ones held between their forepaws. It was a thankless task. Their paw pads were bloodied and if they stopped, even for a moment, a white would snap at their legs, drawing blood which mingled with the earth and the dust and congealed in a thick red-brown substance on the ground. The diggers were against the far wall, as many as thirty of them strung along the entire length of the chamber. They pawed at the face of the wall attempting to remove bits of rocks. Sometimes a larger one would break free. These were shunted away. The whites patrolled the face snapping at any who ceased their labour.

Marsha was horrified. The browns were emaciated, blinded, choking, never daring to look round. And all the time his mind was taking in the scene. Three whites, at the face, two examining specimens, one at the smashing process, three milling around, keeping an eye on proceedings. Nine in all. He counted the browns. There were forty-three.

'Is this the entire workforce?' he asked Para.

'Yes, some have died or been killed off and not yet replaced by leverets. The numbers are constantly changing.'

'And the whites down there examining the rocks. I take it they're looking for the ice rocks.'

Para nodded. 'They keep a hoard of them somewhere near the whites' quarters.'

The work continued for a while. Then one of the whites called a halt. The browns slumped to the ground, breathing heavily and licking their wounds. Nine fresh whites entered the chamber, took up their positions while the others left, and the order was given for the work to recommence.

'How often do the whites change guard like that?' Marsha asked.

'Three times a day.'

'And where are the rest of the whites?'

'Some would be guarding the breeding area; the elite fighters among them form the terror squad, they could be anywhere now; and some would be resting in the whites' quarters.'

'Para, tell us where all those exits lead, give us a general layout of the whole area. Packo, Lotto, listen carefully. It is essential that we familiarise ourselves with everything.'

Para spent several minutes explaining in detail the entire geography of the area. He pointed out the various tunnels which led to the different sections. One led to the whites' quarters up nearer the surface. Another led deeper into the mountain, where lay the browns' quarters. The breeding area was reached by means of another tunnel.

Two tunnels led directly to the outside and the remaining tunnel, near to where the examination of the rocks was taking place, led to the Cavern of Bones. That was where the punishments were carried out and the browns were left to die. Any brown entering that tunnel was never seen again.

'Right,' Marsha said, 'we've seen enough, let's go and join the others.'

Para led them away. They travelled the deserted tunnels gradually working their way down. It appeared that Para had the entire system engrained in his mind. Not once did he falter. He wove in and out of the tunnels, never staying in one very long. He was making it extremely difficult for anyone to follow them.

Finally they emerged into a small chamber with four exits leading off in various directions. Para stopped in his tracks as he peered ahead.

'Oh no,' he whispered.

He moved forward allowing the others to gaze in. At the far

end of the chamber lay two browns. Fresh blood covered their mutilated bodies, their eyes held the vacant stare of death.

'Snappo and Tamol,' Para whispered, 'they must have been found by the terror squad. I thought that they would be safe here. The whites must be extending the areas of their search for us.' He fell silent, aching with the loss of his two friends.

Suddenly, there was a sound away to their left. Each hare spun round immediately, ready to face the whites. It was then that they heard the whimpering. Turna appeared.

'Snappo and Tamol arrived before me,' he mumbled, 'must have been all over in seconds. When I arrived I heard Swengli laughing coarsely, summoning the whites away to fresh killing. There was nothing I could do. I hid.'

He sobbed, ashamed of his inability to save his friends, wishing that he too might have died to put an end to the misery which hung over him. Lotto comforted him, pressing his huge body against Turna's fragile frame.

'Don't worry, little one,' he spoke softly, 'you're going to be free, free from fear — that I promise you.'

Turna gazed at him. He wanted so badly to believe. He felt a great heaviness, the accumulated tiredness of one who has lived long, striven hard, and spent a long time running rarely finding an opportunity to stop. Old age before its time. He had just completed his second summer. Para bit into the nape of Snappo's neck, and dragged his body towards one of the exits and laid it gently to one side. The others stood back. This was something which they knew Para wanted to do alone. They respected that. He took Tamol's body and laid it alongside Snappo's, their final resting place. He stood silently over them for a few moments before turning to the others. 'This is not a safe refuge any more,' he said, 'we'll have to move. Be alert, the whites could still be in the vicinity.'

He plunged into one of the exits, the rest followed. Lotto stayed close to Turna, ready to protect him should the need arise. They travelled for some time at a pace which was far too fast for Para and Turna. The deaths of Snappo and Tamol were obviously on Para's mind. Marsha brought up the rear, his ears attuned to the minutest of foreign sounds. He heard nothing. Lotto was about to ask Para to call a halt for the sake of Turna, who was hardly able to catch his breath, when Para stopped. 'In here,' he panted. Packo went in first. There was a short passageway which opened out into a small recess, five paces deep, three wide. They all assembled inside. Turna was retching, his body racked in pain. Para was little better.

'Rocks, there, by the entrance.' Para spat the words out. Packo pushed two rocks into the passageway. They did not close the space completely, rather they hid the occupants and rendered the recess inaccessible. Marsha was not pleased with the hiding place. They were trapped, one way in, one way out. It contravened all his principles of safe hiding. However, he didn't argue the point. Turna, clearly, could travel no further for some time; Para also was very weak. 'Get some sleep,' he ordered, 'I'll keep watch.' He settled down beside one of the rocks blocking the entrance.

Lotto stayed with Turna. All the terrible injustice and suffering of this Land of Deep Shadow was before him, epitomised in this frail, timid hare. He was becoming angry

'I . . . think . . . we'll . . . be safe . . . here,' Para struggled to speak.

'Don't worry,' Marsha assured him, 'please, rest.' Para obediently squatted on the ground.

'Want some company?' Packo asked, settling down beside Marsha.

Marsha smiled. 'I'd be glad of some inspiration,' he said, 'any ideas?'

'You mean, am I "seeing" anything?'

Marsha nodded.

'Afraid not.'

'You'll see when you need to,' Marsha told him. 'Anyway, we know why we're here. The question is, how can the three of us best help the browns. Some place this, isn't it?'

'It sure is,' Packo agreed. 'You know, now I'm here, I feel very strongly that I'll never leave.'

Marsha narrowed his eyes. Was this some dreadful premonition of death?

'Packo, get some rest, I'll call you later to take over. Let's leave Lotto with Turna, he can serve a better purpose there.' Packo settled down. He recognised that Marsha wanted to think quietly.

Marsha sat, gazing into the space between the rocks. He began to consider all the terrible sights he had seen this day. Time passed. Slowly, like a cloud passing unhurriedly across the sky, a plan began to form in his mind. The more he pondered the more he realised that if they were to repulse the whites and bring freedom to the browns, they would have to be willing to take the ultimate risk. That ultimate risk involved the highest stake they had to offer — their lives.

Chapter Seventeen

Marsha continued the watch throughout most of the night. He did not feel tired, yet he realised that he must sleep. He would need his wits about him in the days ahead. He prodded Packo. It was then that he heard the noise, a low groan. Did it emanate from the recess or from beyond? He glanced over at Lotto. Turna moved slightly. Lotto was awake immediately, stroking his coat. Turna relaxed. Then, there was another sound, not a groan this time but a padding of paws some way off down one of the tunnels. That could mean only one thing, the terror squad.

He quickly prodded Packo again and this time he woke. Marsha motioned to him to remain silent and pointed to the rocks. The padding paws had advanced nearer and could be heard strengthening in intensity all the time. Marsha crouched beside the rocks, Packo did likewise. They waited.

They came very close, seven or eight whites. They gathered outside the recess. A voice boomed through the silence. It was the voice they had heard before, the one that had mocked them and called them cowards, that had warned them that there would be no mercy. Marsha and Packo lay perfectly still, Lotto was awake, aware, a paw on Turna's neck. Para slept, oblivious of it all.

'This is about the end of it,' Swengli was saying. 'This tunnel leads outside. They've gone. Don't worry lads, it's only a matter of time. Just remember, that big one, he's mine. I'll enjoy ripping his ears off first.'

'What about this, boss?' A white was sniffing around the entrance to the recess, his snout twitching.

Swengli looked in and noticed the rocks. He hesitated. Had he noticed something else? Marsha readied himself. A long, long, moment passed.

'It's just another tunnel,' he growled, 'we don't want to get lost down there. Listen lads, we'll have them, we always do. Those other browns, the strangers, they won't last long. They're inferior to us, cowards. They can't hope to do us any harm. But what will we do to them lads, what will we do to them?'

The whites laughed. Swengli was psyching them up, allaying the disappointment of a fruitless search, assuring them that it represented merely a stay of execution.

'Come on lads, let's get back and have a look at the biggest ice rock we've ever found. I tell you, lads, when that arrives home we'll all be heroes. We've got it made.'

Packo took over the watch and Marsha slept. Para woke him some time later. 'We should move,' he said.

Marsha was awake in an instant and completely aware of his surroundings. 'We're safe here,' he told Para, 'this area has been searched and we were not discovered.'

'You mean there was a terror squad here, while we slept?' Para sounded incredulous.

Lotto approached. 'Turna's dead,' he said simply. 'He passed away quietly in his sleep. He's out of it now.'

Para dropped his head. 'Poor Turna, the latest victim.' He looked at them. 'You know, I remember well the first time he was ever in the open air, after he had escaped with me. He had dreamed for so very long about open spaces, fresh air, the wind, rain, snow. When we made our break for freedom he was so excited. When we broke from the overwhelming oppression out into the wide open spaces, he was terrified. He's been frightened ever since. I do believe he died of fright. I should have done more.'

'No,' Lotto told him. 'He woke occasionally during the night. I think he knew he was going to die. His last words were, "Thank

Para for me, he showed me our natural way of life for a little while. I'm not strong enough to grasp it." You have nothing to regret. You see, Turna needed the one thing you couldn't give him, the one thing you didn't have, peace. You cannot have peace if you live in fear. We have to try to remove that fear.'

They placed Turna at the far end of the recess, his hind legs beneath his body, his forepaws stretched out, supporting his head. Packo placed a line of tiny pebbles around the body, marking a perimeter. This was now a sacred area. The line between life and death was as fragile as the line of pebbles. They left him there and respectfully withdrew a few paces.

'You were awake last night, Lotto, when our visitors approached?' Marsha asked.

Lotto nodded.

'You know then that you have made an enemy in Swengli. He wants to rip your ears off, and that's only for starters.'

'When I meet Swengli he'll have more than my ears to worry about.'

'Now, listen,' Marsha began, 'the first thing we need to do is to familiarise ourselves with the network of tunnels around the digging area. We must know them intimately, our lives may depend upon that knowledge. To reconnoitre again is to tempt fate so you must teach us, Para. Let's start with the digging area itself, remind us of what we observed earlier.'

So they began. Para scraped out a rough map on the ground and revised the entire layout and where the tunnels led. Then he began to fan out, taking them through the tunnels themselves, teaching them how to find their way about.

'Always remember two rights and a left and you'll never get lost,' he concluded.

'Sounds simple enough,' Lotto said.

'Ah well, Lotto, there is some bad news.'

'I might have known it,' Lotto said resignedly, 'what is it?'

'For a start, recesses like this. Occasionally a tunnel might lead to a dead end. Such tunnels are always very short, however, and you would soon realise it. Also, some of the tunnels do become narrow at times, you would have to watch that, Lotto.'

'I'll bear that in mind,' Lotto smiled.

'Now,' Marsha stood, 'how about some food? We're near the outside here, aren't we?'

'Yes,' Para replied, 'first left.'

'Come on, Packo, we'll see what we can find.'

Lotto removed the rocks only sufficiently for them to squeeze through and then replaced them. Marsha and Packo returned within minutes. Lotto thought that they were whites at first and he crouched behind the rocks.

'Hey, Lotto,' Packo shouted, 'move the rocks.'

They were white with snow and in their mouths they carried grass shoots. They didn't bother to shake themselves off.

'You can collect the snow off us,' Marsha said, 'it will provide a little moisture. Or you can pop outside and stand in it. The snows have arrived in a big way.'

'And the winds too,' Packo informed them, 'it's blowing a gale out there.'

They chewed at the grass shoots which provided them with some nourishment. Marsha waited until they had finished.

'Time to make plans,' Marsha announced. 'The terror squad spent the night searching for us.'

'Correct,' Para concurred, 'and if they have searched this mountain then tonight they'll go further afield. They will expect us to follow our normal pattern and be out and about at night.'

'And we shall not disappoint them. Hopefully though they will expect us to be out there somewhere. We must give them time to leave and then strike.'

'What exactly have you in mind, Marsha?' Lotto asked.

'The way I see it is this . . .'

▲▼▲

The time had come. They had spent a restless day, fidgeting, wanting the daylight hours to pass, and yet not wanting them to pass. Marsha realised that his plan needed precise timing. He did not wish to contend with the terror squad, not just yet. Therefore, they had to wait. He only hoped that his conclusions about the terror squad were correct and that they would be well out of earshot. Now he decided that the time was right. He squeezed past the rocks, ran up the tunnel, and emerged into the open air. It had stopped snowing, the stars were beginning to twinkle as night fell. He returned to the hideout.

'To the diggings,' he told the others, 'you all know what to do.'

They filed from the recess. Lotto carefully replaced the rocks. 'This one's for you, Turna,' he whispered into the darkness. Para led the way. Packo followed, resolutely. Lotto was third and Marsha brought up the rear. Para followed a direct route. They had to be at the diggings well before work finished for the day.

As they approached they caught the sound of breaking rocks; the occasional anguished cry of a beaten brown; the sharp, shrill orders of the guards. As they gazed at the pitiful scene once again, this time from a side tunnel, they felt the same revulsion, the same tug at their hearts, the same searing sense of injustice, the same determination. Now they were to act; it was the time.

Marsha nodded and each stole to his position, hidden still from prying eyes.

The work continued. This was a day like any other and the quota had to be met. The amount of digging, sifting, and sorting that that entailed was known only to the whites. The browns, without hope, forlorn, heads lowered, forequarters hunched, went about their tasks as usual. This was their humdrum way of life. Little did they know that it was all about to change.

Marsha charged to centre stage.

'Freedom!' he cried, 'Freedom!'

The browns paused from their labours, stared at him incredulously, and then at each other. The whites also stared, as astonished at this turn of events as their captives.

It was exactly the response that Marsha had anticipated. Grand drama for a grand occasion. No one could have done it better! Before anyone moved Packo and Lotto charged onward from different points. Packo delivered a telling blow to one of the whites at the digging face. Lotto was even more effective. He appeared from the shadows, huge and threatening. He approached the opposite end of the digging face and delivered a blow of such stunning power that he sent his victim careering into the flank of another white, bowling him over. As the shock of the attack reverberated around the site Marsha was on the move. He smacked the white who had been bullying the rock rollers, and while he was still dazed he unleashed a tremendous hind leg kick to the ribs. Packo and Lotto were also moving on. Packo took out the remaining work face guard while Lotto streaked across to the rock examiners and clattered their open-mouthed heads together.

Only five seconds had passed. The captive browns were stunned. Then pandemonium broke out. The browns surged towards the centre attacking the remaining two whites, showering them with weak blows. The whites reacted swiftly, killing several of their emaciated assailants before Marsha, Packo and Lotto were able to get to the centre themselves and dispatch the whites. Now the fury of the browns knew no bounds. They had been held in slavery all of their lives, terrified by the whites. They fought frantically to rain a blow on an unconscious white.

Now Para leapt into the thick of the action. He was recognised immediately. 'Quickly,' he shouted, 'to the whites' quarters: it is a forbidden area no longer.'

It had all gone nearly as Marsha had planned. Overpower the guards at the digging area, hope that the browns respond, and then, before the euphoria dies, launch an attack on the whites' living quarters. He had not anticipated, however, that the browns would tackle the whites as they had. There was much work still to do.

Lotto was already at the appropriate tunnel as the browns, led by Para, charged towards it. He began to lope down. A second left, first right, straight stretch, then follow the tunnel as it curved away to the left. He veered left with the curve. The browns were not yet in view behind him. It was strangely quiet, suddenly he felt very much alone. An image of Crust flashed through his mind. 'Go wiv the blow, stick one on the snout, make their eyes pop out!' That would surely be his advice now. It would have been great to have the little fellow here, tearing alongside. 'Cam on, Lotto, let's giv em 'ell.' An apt description of this hopeless place.

Then, six or seven paces ahead, a white appeared. He looked at Lotto, wondering what was going on. Here was a huge brown bearing down upon him. That moment of astonishment was all Lotto required. He raced forward and delivered a thunderous blow to the snout.

'Good on yer, Lotto. Giv im wot for.'

The white slumped to the ground. Lotto jumped over him and entered a large chamber. Whites were scattered around lying prostrate, resting after their latest round of bullying. Lotto surveyed the scene.

'What do you think you're doing?'

A white at the far end of the chamber stood and stared. His voice was gruff, his words clipped.

'Hey, lads,' he shouted, 'we've got an intruder.'

The whites raised their heads lazily and gazed at Lotto through sleepy eyes.

The white turned back to Lotto. 'You woppos are not allowed here, this is out of limits. We're going to give you a good hiding, that will teach you.'

They moved forward, daring Lotto to make a break for it or to cower. They were three paces in front of him when the onslaught arrived. Para appeared, then another brown, and then another. They hurtled into the chamber charging at the whites.

Lotto plunged into the fray. The whites, staggering under the initial attack, were regrouping and now were beginning to punish the weaker browns. The browns' attack was headstrong and lacked discipline, their strength did not match their frenzy. The sixteen whites were not only holding their own, they were gaining the upper hand. Lotto waded in, lashing mighty blows to any white near him. He quickly reached the far wall leaving in his wake a line of dazed whites whom the browns quickly finished off. And there, whisker to whisker, he met the haughty white who had challenged him. Now he could see the fear in the eyes of the white, a white long used to blind obedience and terror in those who stood before him.

Lotto wasted no time. He smashed his right forepaw into the white's jaw, then thumped his left down on top of his head. The white passed out. Then, above all the din, he heard a shrill scream. Lotto turned and saw a thin, sickly looking brown crying out in agony as a white beat him. He raced over, his momentum slamming the white against the wall with a tremendous thud. The brown was panting. He looked up and smiled, then closed his eyes for the last time.

Lotto felt the rage welling up inside him. There was no sense to all this brutality and he determined that these whites were going to discover that when the situation is reversed, violence is not such a favourable option. He tore into the attack, rescuing browns, throwing whites aside.

Marsha had also plunged in, making himself available to protect the weaker browns. He found that as soon as he managed to throw a decent blow which stunned one of the whites, the browns' courage would increase and they would snap and hit out at the beleaguered white.

Marsha's plan had left Packo to the rear. His task was to watch for the return of the terror squad and also to deal with any whites who emerged from the chamber. Two did find their way out, escaping from the confined chaos. He dealt with them swiftly. He kept a vigilant eye both on the tunnel and on the chamber itself. Occasionally he rushed in to fling a blow at a white who was pressing hard on a brown. After a while, with Marsha and Lotto in full flight, it became obvious that the whites would soon be overcome. He decided to investigate some of the tunnels they had passed. In the very first opening he reached, he spotted something of interest. It looked like a pile of rocks heaped against a wall. He stole in and touched the pile with his paw. It was cold and hard. He scratched and a few of the rocks fell from the heap. He picked one up and examined it. It was like ice and yet, as he turned it, it almost seemed to glow, to change colour. 'So,' he thought, this is what all this savagery is about.' He tossed it toward the tunnel entrance. Suddenly he felt a flash of inspiration. He tossed another, then another. He worked frantically until he had nearly half the pile stocked by the entrance. He pushed his way out and ran back to the whites' quarters. The battle was over. The whites had been overcome. The defeat, however, had been costly. They had taken a ghastly revenge on the pitiful browns. Many were dead or injured. The survivors were totally exhausted. Packo approached Marsha.

'We're stuck here for a while, I'm afraid,' Marsha told him. 'As soon as it's possible we'll move out. We must free the does and leverets before the terror squad returns. Para will show us a safe place to hide.'

'I'll keep watch,' Packo said. Within minutes Packo was back. 'Bad news. The terror squad, returning early.'

'That's all we need.' Marsha called Lotto over and indicated that he should follow them. Out in the tunnel they could clearly detect the sound of voices, more importantly there was no sense of urgency. Obviously they had not been to the digging area and were not aware that anything was wrong. Packo had pushed half a dozen ice rocks into the tunnel. He approached them now. 'This is what we'll do,' he whispered.

Marsha and Packo crouched against the rock walls, their natural colour blending in and camouflaging them perfectly against an early sighting. They hardly need have worried. As they came ever nearer, their clipped voices raised, the whites appeared intent on only one thing, sleep.

They were between five and ten paces away. Packo jumped from his hiding place, Marsha did likewise. Packo took up an ice rock, aimed, and threw. It smashed into the leading white. Marsha threw a split second later. His aim was not as true, luckily his rock ricocheted off the tunnel walls and thudded down upon another white. They maintained a steady barrage. Lotto was concealed in the tunnel pushing the rocks out.

The whites had been shocked by the initial assault. The rocks were showering down at them. The leading four had fallen, their bodies spread-eagled on the rough ground. Six whites crouched behind them waiting for the bombardment to end.

Marsha and Packo stood back and took stock. Lotto had kept them amply supplied with ammunition and the ice rocks lay strewn before them. They too crouched and waited. The silence hung like a pall of smoke. Moments became like hours as the battle of wits stretched. The whites had been taken by surprise. Their haughtiness began to return. They were the terror squad, the elite. They could not be overpowered so easily. They would wait just a little longer, allow the silence to get to the browns, allow the terror to seep back into them.

Then, abruptly, it came. The whites charged in unison, shrieking, their cries reverberating around the tunnel, beating from wall to wall like a bird trapped in a glass cage. Packo sprang up immediately, oblivious to the explosion of noise. He threw a rock which stunned one of the front runners. Marsha, although reacting with lightning speed, did not have the opportunity to release a rock before the whites were upon them. Lotto charged out of the side tunnel pushing a bemused white hard against the wall. He fell forward, stumbling over the body of a white Marsha had knocked unconscious. Another white jumped on top of him forcing the air from his lungs. Marsha and Packo pressed forward thudding punches on Lotto's assailant. Yet another white had rushed at Lotto and buried his teeth in one of his hind legs. Marsha struck out sideways catching him below the eye and forcing him to release his grip. Lotto was immediately on his feet delivering a deluge of blows.

Suddenly there was only one white left. He stood back and glared at them, hatred dripping from his mad eyes. Lotto looked up and caught Swengli's malicious stare. Then, without a word, Swengli turned and was gone.

'Quickly,' Marsha shouted, 'we mustn't allow him to get to the breeding quarters.'

They had learned the route off by heart. Swengli had disappeared from view, swerving into a side tunnel to his left.

'Lotto, you follow him, we'll take the main route to the breeding quarters.' Marsha shouted the orders tersely.

Marsha and Packo arrived at the breeding quarters. They found three startled whites standing guard. They dealt with them swiftly. No sign of Swengli. The does gazed at them, disbelief spread across their faces. The leverets slept peacefully. Then they heard the sound. The unmistakable padding of paws, the heavy breathing of one who had run hard. They readied themselves for the savage Swengli. Lotto plodded into view.

'I lost him, slowed by the injury to the leg. I had a feeling that he was heading for an outside exit so I made my way there. I spotted him well off in the distance, charging away. He's gone.'

'He'll be back,' Packo spoke in that faraway voice. 'When he returns the final battle will be fought.'

Chapter Eighteen

Swengli was the only white to survive the uprising. The browns who had managed to come through unscathed were soon restored to another burst of energy after their efforts in the whites' quarters and they rampaged through the tunnels. Their newfound freedom won expression in discovering dazed whites. Their retribution was swift, especially against any of the terror squad who had not perished in the encounter with Marsha, Packo, and Lotto.

The cost of the initial surge for freedom had been heavy. Only fifteen browns were uninjured. Eighteen had died and ten suffered bites and bruises. They would recover in a few days. It was some time before all the able-bodied, including does and leverets, gathered in the breeding quarters. Para, his fur covered in congealed blood, called for silence.

'Free,' he shouted hoarsely, 'free at last.'

There was a huge cheer.

'And these are our deliverers,' Para announced, pointing to Marsha, Packo, and Lotto.

Another huge cheer. Marsha stepped forward. The din subsided. 'I have bad news,' he said. Absolute silence descended like the dark of a moonless night. 'My friends, you are not free, not yet. Swengli escaped, doubtless he has gone for assistance. He, and perhaps many more, will be back.'

The browns looked at each other timorously, their bravado shattered like a wave smashing against the unyielding cliff face.

'The deep shadow is lifted temporarily.' It was Packo who now spoke. His eyes were far away, his voice eerie. 'The first taste of freedom is bitter-sweet for it is a pleasure that may be short-lived. The threat will come again. When it does you must resolve that you would rather give your lives than return to slavery. The deep shadow can only be removed by sacrifice; better to die in the light than to be cast into the darkness forever. Now we all approach our destiny. We must grasp it.'

He fell silent. Everyone waited, wondering. Then, a young, nearly blind hare, hopped to the centre. 'I'm ready to die,' he whispered. He cleared his throat of the dust that was choking him. 'I'm ready to die,' he said loudly, 'ready to follow if you'll lead.'

'And what is your name?' Marsha asked.

'Sooze.'

'Well, Sooze, one thing is certain, you'll never be a slave again — ever.'

They all milled forward. 'Lead us, lead us,' they shouted eagerly.

'We will lead,' Marsha cried, 'we have much to do. We must prepare for the onslaught. Para, take the browns and tend to the wounded. The whites' quarters are now our quarters. Leave Sooze with us. Lotto, will you assist Para? Sooze, will you show us every area you know, and perhaps even lead us to the areas you don't know?'

Sooze smiled. 'I sure will.'

Marsha turned to the does, 'We must defend ourselves against the whites when they return. Can you gather all the leverets and move them somewhere safe?'

An old doe approached. 'All the leverets are here, eighteen in all.'

Marsha scanned the area. 'But surely they are scattered throughout the tunnels leading away from here.'

'Traditional leveret upbringing was forcibly changed long ago. The whites insisted that our young be raised together. They thought that it would take away their independence, make them afraid to be alone.'

'And did it?' Packo asked.

The old doe chuckled. 'No. nature cannot be changed so easily. The mothers became more determined than ever not to allow their young to become mere automatons. We have always believed that the chance of liberation would come. Against that day we have instilled in them a fierce pride; it will be our major weapon now. We will take our leverets to the next mountain, they will be safe there. If necessary those of us who can fight will return. We will fight for their future.'

'Your name is Stoli,' Packo said.

'And you are the Seer promised us so very long ago,' she murmured thoughtfully.

'I'm not sure what all that means,' Packo replied. 'I don't know. I don't even know how I knew your name.'

The old doe narrowed her eyes and looked at him searchingly. 'I know,' she told him. There was great purpose in her voice. 'You used a special name when you spoke to me, a name known only to a select few until now. My mother passed it on to me before she died. She charged me with the responsibility to pass it on to my last born or surviving doe before I died. It has been thus for countless generations. You have come that we might be free. Hear me well. Freedom can be achieved in one of two ways. The whites might be overcome and we old ones will enjoy peace in our remaining days. Or, we may all die — if not all then many of us. That too will represent freedom. Your presence here does not assure any of us of physical freedom, remember that and do not give those young bucks false hope. They could well be disappointed. And you, Packo, what will become of you? Nothing is preordained. You, of all here, must accept your destiny; the choice is yours.'

Stoli turned away. 'Come, does, collect your leverets, we must travel. Sooze, tell Para that we will be at level three, due east. He'll understand.' She led them away.

Packo stared after her. She had sounded almost like his mother. What exactly was she saying to him?

'Right, Sooze, my young friend,' Marsha spoke loudly and energetically, breaking Packo's trance-like state. 'I want you to take us to every part of this mountain that you know.'

Sooze smiled again, glad to be of service.

'Come, Packo,' Marsha suggested emphatically, 'remember all you see. We need a strategy and we must familiarise ourselves with the territory.'

Some time later they stood together at the now deserted digging area. Sooze had shown them mostly what they had already seen. The only new place they visited was the browns' sleeping quarters. They were damp, musky and cold, another testament to the whites' cruelty.

Sooze pointed to a spot where the rock inspection had taken place. 'We were always told that if we ever entered that tunnel we would never be seen again. If the whites wanted to remove someone they would drag him away through that tunnel. You went through there to die. Somewhere through that tunnel is what we call the Cavern of Bones.'

'Would you like to show us?' Marsha asked softly.

Sooze took them as far as the tunnel entrance. 'I'm not sure that I'm ready to go through there just yet,' he said.

'That's fine. Wait for us here, Sooze, we won't be long.'

Marsha and Packo entered the tunnel. Immediately the ground began to drop, the air became colder and their eyes watered. And there was something else. There were no tunnels to right or left. The way was straight and steep and it was carrying them further and further into the depths. Even the odour changed. It was rank and fetid and filled with death. Marsha's fur began to rise on his back. There was a presence here, threatening and sinister. This was an abode of lurking evil.

The tunnel opened into a large chamber. At the far end, perhaps fifteen paces distant, a black semi-circular pool of water was occasionally disturbed as a drip from the wet rock above fractured its surface. Now they were at the very centre of the decay and rottenness. The entire chamber was flooded with white bones. Skulls of long-dead hares were propped up in makeshift fashion on long thin bones. The empty cavities from where eyes had once surveyed the world drew their vision like magnets. The very silence was frightening. Only the intermittent plop of water disturbing the black sheet causing quiet ripples to enliven the dead water momentarily could be heard. All around lay the chaos of bones carpeting the ground in a thick pile.

'Urrrr . . .'

Simultaneously they froze. The sound came from the far edge of the chamber. Whoever, whatever, was hidden by the profusion of bones. The deathly hush returned. Plop, the drip again disturbed the sheet.

'Urrrr . . .'

Fainter this time, but now they were prepared to home in on the noise. Marsha pinpointed the exact location. He stared hard. He could see nothing. He tossed his head indicating that Packo should take the left. He moved to the right, disturbing the bones in the process, clattering them together. It was impossible to stalk. He haunched his body, hesitatingly. Packo did likewise.

'Please . . . come.'

The voice was weak but unmistakably pleading. This was no trick.

'Marsha, Packo, where are you?' It was Para followed by Lotto and Sooze. They burst into the chamber. Para stood, gasping for breath, hardly believing his eyes, seeing the place for the first time and realising what an apt description 'Cavern of Bones' was.

'Sooze . . . told me . . . you came . . . here,' Para struggled to speak. 'Cavern of Bones . . . evil . . . come away.'

His expression was wide-eyed, terror stricken. 'Away . . . away . . .'

'There's someone alive over here,' Marsha told him simply, 'he needs our help.' Marsha turned back to the prostrate white, his eyes once more held captive by the dreadful sight. Both ears had been viciously bitten off. One eye was completely closed, the other bloodied. Deep welts ran along his flanks. Dried blood and dirt stayed the flow of blood. He lay awkwardly, the slightest movement torture. His hind legs protruded from his body grotesquely, both broken and useless.

'My friend,' Marsha said gently, 'did Swengli do this to you?'

'Yes.' As he opened his mouth Marsha noticed that the teeth had been broken. 'Never mind.' His voice was low and very weak. His head slumped back to the ground.

'Primo, Primo, what have they done to you?' Para had clambered over the bones and gazed at the forlorn body. 'Who is he?' Marsha asked, struggling to keep his voice calm.

'A friend to us,' Para replied brokenly. 'Primo helped us escape. He told us, often, that not all whites are evil. He deplored the injustice here and assisted us whenever he could.'

'Swengli must have found out and made an example of him,' Marsha nodded as understanding dawned.

'Where is Swengli?' Primo asked, surprised to be talking to browns.

'Gone,' Marsha assured him, 'we have taken over, only he escaped.'

A smile broke over Primo's pained face. 'I'm glad,' he whispered, 'so very glad. We are not all like him.' His breathing became laboured following the effort he had made to speak.

'Swengli will return,' he began again fighting to utter the words. 'Three, four days' journey home, same back. He will bring the next detachment. You must defeat him, end this barbarity.'

Packo had found a hollow rock and had filled it with water. Carefully he held Primo's head and tipped the contents into Primo's mouth. Primo coughed and spluttered but the cool liquid eased the burning in his throat.

'The ice rocks, they fight for them back home, prestige to own them. The younger generation turn away, reject wanton materialism . . . they grow disenchanted. Such silly games our elders play . . .'

'Don't talk anymore,' Packo told him, 'we'll take care of you.'

'So, you must be the Seer!' Primo relaxed. 'Now I know what Stoli meant when she spoke to me. Here is your destiny, here.'

Primo lowered his head.

Packko was still confused. It seemed so very long ago since his mother had challenged him to find his destiny. Now he had been told by a stranger that his destiny was here. The message now was as oblique as ever.

'He's dead,' Marsha announced.

'Primo, dead!' Sooze had remained on the periphery until now. He stepped forward, looked at the broken body for a moment, and then crouched beside it and began to stroke the fur gently. 'They did this to you because of me. I'm so sorry.' He was very distressed.

Marsha and the others stood back, allowing the youngster time, those precious first moments as realisation dawned at the death of a friend. Finally, Sooze rose, cast one last, lingering look at Primo, and then began to gather bones and place them tenderly over the body. He covered it completely, hiding it from the view of prying eyes. He turned and caught Marsha's eye.

'Primo rescued me, he probably saved my life,' Sooze said quietly. 'A few days ago two whites picked on me at the diggings. They accused me of not working hard enough. They started to rough me up. Primo intervened. They picked on him instead. They called him a "brownie lover". He went for them, nearly killed one before others arrived followed by Swengli. Swengli said that he had always had doubts about him, thought that he fraternised with us too much, had too high an opinion of himself. He ordered that Primo be taken to the Cavern of Bones where he personally would take care of him. Primo used to say that when he finished his tour of duty he would fight at home to attempt to put an end to all this evil. He hated his role here. He died because of that hatred.'

'Hatred of evil can only be good,' Packo said. 'We must hate that same evil. It is not the colour of their fur that makes whites evil, rather it is the condition of their hearts. We can take our heart from Primo; we too must seek justice from those whose hearts are evil.'

'And that is what we must be about now,' Marsha emphasised. 'Come, Sooze, we have work to do.'

He led Sooze from the place of torment. The others, with the exception of Packo, followed. He waited until they were gone and then began to cast about, not really knowing what he was looking for. Then his eye was drawn to a dark shape amongst the white bones. He drew the bleached bones apart and there was the body of a brown. Perhaps this was the most recent victim of the terror. The eyes were closed, the hare at peace. Packo watched over him wishing that he might have the gift of life to impart to this forlorn creature. He covered the body. This was a place he did not wish to visit again. Yet, perhaps his destiny *was* here.

The whites' quarters were a veritable hive of activity when Packo arrived there. Marsha had all the browns in attendance and he and Lotto were applying poultices to their eyes using snow to wash them out.

The browns were in high spirits. Their eyes felt a lot better. 'Right,' Marsha shouted, calling for silence. 'Now, can you do something for me?'

'Yes, of course,' the replies came fast and furious.

'Packo, Para, I want the ice rocks carried to the vantage point above the diggings. Spread them around, in piles. All right?'

'Let's go,' Packo complied. They all departed.

'Now, Lotto, let's have a good look at this place.'

'Haven't we seen everything?' Lotto asked.

'Let's search any alcoves or investigate any tunnels leading off this chamber.'

'What are we looking for?' Lotto asked.

'Oh, you'll know when we find it.'

Lotto shrugged. He veered to the left, Marsha took the right. They sniffed and poked and prodded their way around the periphery, meeting at the far end without discovering anything.

'You know, Lotto, I must be losing my touch, I was sure that we'd find something.' Marsha lifted his head and scanned the rock face.

'Perhaps if you were to tell me exactly what we're supposed

to be looking for,' Lotto suggested.

'Yahoo . . . there . . . up there.' Marsha suddenly became very excited.

Lotto studied the rock face. He saw nothing. 'Maybe you are losing your touch,' Lotto said under his breath.

'I heard that,' Marsha laughed. Suddenly he sprang up, flinging himself straight at the rock, four feet or so above them.

Lotto stood back, amazed. He found it difficult to reconcile such antics with the usually serious Marsha. 'I'll have to check the water he's been drinking,' Lotto thought.

But Marsha had disappeared! Lotto re-examined the expanse of rock. At the exact spot Marsha had disappeared there was a slightly darker area. What did that mean? He was given little time to reflect on the situation. He found himself showered with dry grasses, shrivelled berries, still succulent bog cotton shoots, and an assortment of nuts and shoots which Lotto did not recognise. He raised his head. Another shower! By now he was completely covered. Only then did Marsha peer out.

'See,' he shouted down, 'I knew that the whites had to have a food supply somewhere. Here it is. If I'm not mistaken this tunnel is a direct route to the outside thus providing a convenient storage depot. Easy to get the stuff in, and it's lovely and dry. There's enough here to last for months. Go and call Para and the rest, they could do with a good feed, it'll pep them up. And you thought I was losing my marbles.'

'I'm sure it's a great relief to you to know that they are still intact! You just sit there feeling smug, I'll get the others. Let it be a surprise.'

The browns entered the whites' quarters. It was still somewhat strange to do so. They felt like usurpers in their own land. They were hungry and weak, their success in driving the whites out already losing some of its potency.

'Come in! Come in!' Marsha greeted them. 'Eat your fill, you deserve it!'

Their eyes opened wide. A mountain of food lay before them, more food than they had ever seen in their lives. Any feelings of despair soon vanished. They all ate — ate until they were bloated. Then, slowly, they dispersed. The pain in their eyes had gone, they were full and well fed. Everything was right in the world.

'Para, Packo, Lotto,' Marsha called, 'let me tell you what I have planned and what we still have to do. Neither of us knows how long it will be before Swengli returns, six days minimum, possibly more. When he comes we must be ready. This is what I've been thinking . . .'

Chapter Nineteen

A week passed, and then another. Still Swengli did not return. Twenty-five browns had survived, and they were growing restless. They were living in a state of emergency for which there appeared to be no need. Four hares were posted as lookouts: an early warning of Swengli's return was all important. The shifts changed every three hours and those who had completed their duty would gather in the whites' quarters, frozen, their eyes smarting. Marsha had continued to treat their eyes every day and a vast improvement was enjoyed by all.

Marsha was at pains to devise so-called recreational pursuits. In reality he was in deadly earnest. He divided the browns into three groups with Packo, Lotto, and himself as leaders. Diplomatically he had offered leadership to Para but he had declined because he felt that he did not have the experience or the fighting prowess of the newcomers. He attached himself to Marsha and acted as his second in command. It was an arrangement Marsha was more than happy with. If the whites were to be defeated it would take both guile and co-operation. Marsha would provide the guile, only Para could ensure the co-operation.

Lotto led his group with unswerving loyalty. He was already a legend. His mere size saw to that. His fighting prowess was talked about reverentially. Stories of him striding among whites lifting them to right and left circulated with awe. He was mighty and automatically commanded respect. Yet he was so gentle, so kind. These were the qualities which enhanced his reputation.

Packko was regarded as different. Rumour had it that he was the Seer, the chosen one. It was felt that he could not be understood, but to be near him might somehow afford one the opportunity to be privy to some special message. Although Packo himself was unaware of it, he possessed an aura to which the browns were attracted.

Marsha planned that these three groups should act as three independent units when the whites returned. Each had to know what was expected of them. Three groups fighting independently, functioning as one unit. Each day the groups worked together. Marsha had them 'play' an innocuous game of hide and seek. Two hares from each group would be given a head start and the rest would have to attempt to catch them. If the two who had led off managed to find their way back to the starting point without being caught they were declared the winners. The game achieved two important ends. The first was that the browns began to attain a decent level of fitness. They were using their limbs, running fast, and feeling their lungs burst. The second was that the browns now had an opportunity to find their way around, to discover, at first hand, their surroundings.

Marsha also devised what he called 'operational exercises'. He laid great emphasis on the initial attack and the browns' ability to cope with it. If they could succeed in throwing the whites into some kind of confusion and disarray then they might gain the upper hand. Certainly they had to use the element of surprise to their own advantage and let the whites know that reconquest was to be no mere formality. Each group had a position carefully selected at the end of one of the tunnels overlooking the digging area. They practised assembling there and racing to it from various locations. Marsha also wanted to acclimatise them to being out in the open and for part of each day they would venture out and throw snowballs at one another. That was great fun. Crust had taught Packo to throw, it would be a useful weapon in the armoury. The does and leverets were visited daily by one of the groups. As well as ensuring that they did not feel neglected it was another method of exercising, and one that entailed travelling some distance in open terrain.

Despite the activities and the plentiful food supply, real freedom had not yet been achieved. This was the curse that plagued them. The threat of the deep shadow remained. The browns wanted to abandon this mountain and establish a new home elsewhere. Marsha knew that that was not the answer. The deep shadow would follow them wherever they went. Real freedom would involve the ultimate confrontation with the whites. They would come to reclaim the land, their slaves, and, above all, the ice rocks. This was to be the final battlefield.

Agitation continued to grow and finally Marsha decided to address them all. Only the lookouts were absent. What he had to say would filter through to them soon enough.

'We all know that Swengli will return,' he told them. 'Swengli knows that we are expecting him. He is playing on that. The longer he stays away, keeps us waiting, the more brittle he hopes we'll become. He has miscalculated. The longer he waits, the stronger we become, the more resolute. You have suffered long and hard. Do not give in, now that freedom is so close. We can win this war. If we stay together we can win.'

A cheer rang round the assembled browns. They would remain buoyant for a few more days.

'Do you believe we can win?' Lotto asked quietly.

'I have to, Lotto, and so do you.'

'Sooze,' Packo called, 'let's check on the lookouts, see if there's anything to report.'

'Sure,' Sooze replied. He had become Packo's second. He followed his leader everywhere and was always willing.

They travelled to the highest lookout first, the one which surveyed the northern territory. They found Aldo there, a young contemporary of Sooze.

'How's it going, Aldo?' Sooze asked.

'Quiet, as usual,' the hare replied, his teeth chattering against the cold. They peered across the landscape. It was frozen white, gleaming in a watery afternoon sun. They sat quietly for several moments. Then, abruptly, Packo sat up: 'There's something out there.' Sooze and Aldo glanced at each other nervously.

'Where exactly?' Sooze asked.

Packo remained transfixed, staring out into the vastness. Then he turned to Sooze. 'Go back to Marsha,' he told him, 'tell him I'm leading someone in by the main arterial route from the north. Tell him to be ready.'

'What are you going to do?' Sooze asked.

'Act as decoy. Now, go! Aldo, stay here, keep up the good work.'

Packo plunged forward past the startled Aldo and began careering down the steep snowy slope. Aldo followed Packo's precarious descent then looked out to scan the countryside. Still he saw nothing.

What had Packo seen out there? It was just a glimpse of a movement. And what he had seen he hardly dared believe. Now the compulsion was upon him. He had to get down to see whether or not his eyes had deceived him.

When Aldo returned his gaze once more to where he thought Packo ought to be, Packo had disappeared. Aldo wondered and feared that perhaps Packo had been in too much of a hurry. The mountains were doubly dangerous at this time of year; failure to respect them could be fatal.

▲▼▲

'So, Packo wants us to prepare to meet him at the lower entrance,' Marsha said thoughtfully.

'Yes, and he said to warn you to be ready,' Sooze added.

'Anything else?'

'No.'

'Well, we'd better set to then.'

A panting brown raced into the digging area where Marsha had been taking the message from Sooze. 'Someone coming,' he burst out, 'lower entrance.'

'Sooze,' Marsha called, reacting to the news immediately, 'call Lotto, I think he's on the higher levels with his group. Para, collect our group and have them assemble at the lower entrance. I'll go there directly.'

▲▼▲

Packo quickly discovered that he was travelling at a speed that was reckless. The mountain snow was frozen fast and the surface gleamed meanly. He lost control, his legs buckled beneath him, and he slid down the ice sheet faster and faster until he reached a short ledge. Suddenly he was flying. He had landed before he fully appreciated what was happening. His paws jabbed through the frozen topmost layer and broke into the softer snow beneath, which had drifted several feet deep in the hollow in which Packo now found himself. He had been lucky. From now on he would pick his steps more gingerly. He had very nearly reached the valley floor. Boulders lay strewn round about him and he began to negotiate a path between them. Soon he would be on level ground and heading north, exactly the route Swengli had taken. He strode on, down the remainder of the slope and onto the valley floor. He stopped and glanced around. Something was wrong! Suddenly, in his mind's eye, the scene he had viewed earlier so vividly flashed before him. He had arrived. There was nothing here!

Then he heard the sound, like a pebble rolling roughly over an uneven surface. There was no time to think, the dark shape was upon him, punching, kicking, hitting home weak blows.

'Crust, Crust, it's me, Packo.'

Crust stood before him. His eyes flamed, his skin caught tightly round his ribs. 'Packo!' he whispered hoarsely, 'Packo!' He collapsed.

'You're among friends now,' Packo told him, 'catch your breath and I'll show you.'

Marsha stared out at the great white expanse confronting him. Two hares were picking their way towards him. Packo he recognised immediately. His companion stumbled, fell heavily, rose ponderously to his feet, and gamely struggled on. Marsha rushed out. 'Crust, Crust, it *is* you!'

Crust, despite his emaciated condition and dazed state, managed a smile. 'Knew yer couldn't cope wivout me,' he said. He gazed around, trying desperately to focus his watering eyes. 'Where is 'e? The big fellah,' he asked.

'Right here,' Lotto replied pushing his way towards him, 'get on.' Lotto crouched and Crust climbed on to his back.

'Straight to the whites' quarters,' Marsha ordered, 'let's give him a feed.'

Crust ate ravenously. He munched the dried grasses and berries, chewed on the odd nut, and for once experienced that something was indeed more important than talking. Finally he was sated. He looked around with huge hanging eyes. 'Gotta lot t' tell yer but it can keep, need a bit a shuteye.' There, in front of them all, he fell asleep.

He woke several hours later to find Lotto sitting patiently by his side.

'Bin there long, mate?' he asked, yawning.

'I was beginning to wonder whether you'd ever wake up,' Lotto replied.

'Any grub?'

'As much as you can eat.' Lotto pushed grass shoots and berries in front of him.

'Great! Listen, I'll tuck int' this, Lotto. You go an' fetch the uvers an' I'll fill yer all in.'

'My pleasure,' Lotto beamed, 'feeling better?'

'Right as rain, me ole mate, right as rain.'

'It's great to see you again, a real bonus.'

'Yeah, likewise.' Crust lowered his eyes sheepishly. 'Naw, go an' get the uvers before I turn all sentimental like.'

Lotto was back in double quick time, Marsha and Packo in attendance.

'Right,' Crust began, swallowing a couple of berries, 'got some fings t' tell yer, might be important. Briefly, this is wot 'appened. I fell down the scree, remember, when we was gettin' on the trundler. Gave me 'ead a right ole wollop. When I began t' come to the trundler was a winding speck on the 'orizon. Me 'ead was fumpin' like a rabbit wiv a twitch in 'is leg. Om lyin' there wonderin' wot t' do when the ole fellah turns up. "You've had a bit of a fall," 'e says in that distant lah-de-dah way of 'is. "Not to worry," 'e goes on, "you can take the next trundler, it will be along in two days." Well! I can tell yer, I brightened up a fair bit. "You must remember one thing," 'e says, "stay on the trundler until it stops for the second time. Do you understand?" Very insistent 'e was. Then 'e disappeared like a puff of smoke. Next time I see 'im I intend to tell 'im about that, very disconcertin' it is.

'So I wait. When the trundler comes along I jump on, an' then I wait again. I don't know 'ow long I was on it. It stopped once an' the 'ead was changed. Yer know, the front bit. This new one 'ad no smoke billowin' out of it. Anyway, not long now I fought t' meself. Lo an' be 'old, on an' on it goes, days an' nights. An' the cold! Went clean frew me. Eventually the trundler grinds to a 'alt an' off I 'op. It was some sorta 'eaders' settlement. The cold was awful an' I 'adn't eaten for days. I 'ad a stroke of fortune then. I found some grain leakin' from a sack. I filled meself up an' off I fled into the countryside.

'Again I lost track of time. I 'uddled in makeshift forms durin' the day an' travelled at night, wiv not a clue as t' where I was goin'. I ran straight into trouble. Yer not goin' t' believe this. I came across a colony of white 'ares. Stumbled almost straight into em. There was a Parliament on, sixty or more of 'em, arguing. One lad wiv a mesmerisin' sorta voice was urgin' war, an' 'e 'ad plenty of supporters. A group did oppose 'im an' it ended up in a right ole ding dong of a fight I can tell yer.'

Marsha, Packo, and Lotto listened, stunned. Crust had discovered the whites' homeland. He had actually witnessed Swengli's attempts to raise an army. Crust, oblivious to their thoughts, or their widening stares, carried on.

'Then, one of 'em spots me. "Kill 'im, kill 'im," the guvner shouts. "Friendly git," I thought t' meself, but I didn't 'ang about. Before they 'ad grouped I was gone. l can tell yer, they chased me 'ard. If I 'adn't bin so 'ungry an' weak I would 'ave soon left 'em, no bovver. As it was, two of 'em began t' close on me. I dropped outta sight at the top of a 'ill. As they approached I let fly wiv a couple of rocks. Fair knocked the stuffin' out of 'em, I can tell yer. They rolled back down careerin' into the pack followin'. Pity I couldn't 'ave stuck round t' watch. But yer know wot I've always said, never gloat, know wot I mean? I raced off an' saw no more of 'em. That was the last contact I 'ad wiv anyone 'til I jumped Packo. Delirious I was, fought they was still after me. So, I've arrived. Good 'ere innit?' He looked expectantly at their faces. They were silent.

'How many whites opposed the one doing the agitating?' Marsha asked.

'Not many. No way was they gonna win.'

'How many days ago?'

'Four or five, why?'

'Because that army out there are coming after us, and I can tell you one thing, their intentions are not friendly.'

'Blaw-dy 'ell!'

Chapter Twenty

Four days later the whites came. The lookout to the north heard them before he saw them. They were shrieking and bellowing and screaming abuse. They marched in a solid phalanx, heading directly towards the entrance nearest to their old quarters. As they came nearer the browns grew timid. Marsha viewed them, while they were still two hundred paces distant. He had not anticipated this brazen assault, but he recognised it for the clever ploy it was. Swengli was coming with the maximum amount of terror. And the plan was working.

'Get to your positions,' he ordered, 'and try not to be frightened, that's exactly what Swengli wants.'

But where was Swengli? He was not leading this column. Marsha took a quick count. Twenty whites! There had to be more! Were these to be the sacrificial offering? Only Swengli possessed the knowledge that there were newcomers amongst the browns who could fight. He probably had not bothered to mention the new arrivals to his troops.

'Lotto, Packo, Para, check the other approaches. Swengli could be leading a surprise attack elsewhere. You know what to do. Lotto, you take the highest. Crust, stay with me, you might have to take a command. Let's move.'

They raced off in various directions. They had practised, hopefully now it was going to pay dividends. Outside the whites continued, their progress unhampered. The groups of browns waited, scattered along the ends of the higher secondary tunnels above the digging area.

Suddenly there was a commotion along two of the tunnels. Packo and Para arrived back almost simultaneously. Nothing to report. Moments later Aldo, from the highest lookout, appeared.

'Lotto sent me,' he gasped, 'whites coming in from the east.'

Marsha had gambled that Swengli would choose the higher route, the most difficult. Lotto would be there to detain him. The battle of wits had begun and Marsha had enjoyed the first minor victory.

'Crust, as soon as we finish here join Lotto.'

'No problem.' He ambled over to Lotto's leaderless group. 'Chins up mates, we're gonna 'ave us a bit a fun.' They smiled, nervously.

They waited again. Then they came. A huge roar preceded them and then the whites milled into the deserted digging area. They had heralded their approach and now they were at the heart of the mountain, the very place they held dear, whence came their supplies of prestigious ice rocks. This was what they wanted, and it was theirs. The timorous browns had fled. Swengli told them that there might be a slight resistance. Well, where was it?

The first ice rock struck one of the whites forcibly at the nape of the neck. Crust had delivered it, his aim as true as ever. The white screeched and collapsed in an untidy heap. Suddenly the whole working area cascaded with missiles which dropped heavily from the ends of the tunnels high above. Pandemonium broke out as the whites ran for cover, hardly knowing in which direction to turn.

It was over in a matter of seconds. Six bodies lay still, four had been wounded, ten had escaped into the protection of the shadows.

'Crust, get to Lotto quickly,' Marsha ordered.

He nodded and tore off, striding boldly up the main tunnel to the very top of the mountain.

'Now, Packo and Para, let's hunt out these whites while they're still wondering what might happen next.'

▲▼▲

It took Crust three minutes to reach Lotto. He found him spread-eagled against the ground, his head protruding out of the tunnel as he gazed into the depths below. He backed into the passage as Crust arrived.

'Marsha sent me t' giv yer a 'and,' Crust smiled.

'How's everything back there?' Lotto asked.

'Worked a charm, didn't it? They didn't know wot 'it 'em.'

'Good. Now Crust, get this side, lie flat. Wait for me to give the word.'

Crust took up his position, lying prostrate on the ground to Lotto's left and slightly back from the opening. Lotto edged near the opening and cautiously peered out. Swengli was twenty paces down, clambering up, the head of a long column of whites snaking its way up the mountain. Lotto inched back in and lay flat. He did not bother to look out again for fear of being observed. He counted slowly to ten.

'Right, Crust,' he whispered, 'let them have it.'

The two hares put their combined weight behind the boulder in front of them and sent it crashing directly into the path of the oncoming group. Swengli reacted instantly, sidestepping the huge rock. It careered past him, catching the first three of his followers and throwing them down the snow-covered scree slope. Lotto and Crust immediately pushed out another, then another. They waited. Unknown to them they had accounted for another three whites. Also unknown to them, Swengli was hiding behind a large overhanging rock.

They continued to wait, listening for any faint sound to disturb the silence of the night. Long moments passed, and then they heard it. The unmistakable sound of frozen snow crunched underfoot.

'Now,' Lotto said.

Together they heaved out their final three boulders. They thundered down, taking the whites by surprise. Two more were sent plummeting to the valley floor.

'Let's go,' Lotto whispered, 'that'll keep them guessing for a while.'

They raced down the tunnel. Swengli's surprise force were pinned down, wondering. The retaking of the mountain was to be no easy task.

▲▼▲

Once the ice rocks had been discharged Marsha led the browns down to the diggings. They ran quickly to the centre ground.

'So, you whites cower,' Marsha taunted them. The response, true to form, brought the whites charging forward. The browns automatically broke into three groups, Lotto's group joining Marsha. The plan was not immediate head-on confrontation but rather frustration. Browns careered off in every direction leaving the whites in momentary indecision. Packo helped them make up their minds.

'You don't even know what to do,' he shouted, 'Swengli must be really hard up to have to rely on you shower.'

Every last one of them glowered at him. Packo was the only brown in sight. He became the target. They converged on him and, as they did so, he issued a deep-throated gurgle of laughter then turned and disappeared from view. They rushed after him.

While Packo led them away the other browns regrouped in the digging area, and waited.

Packo led his pursuers through the tunnels with which he was now thoroughly acquainted. When he considered that sufficient time had elapsed, he led them back to the digging area. Marsha and the rest were there, ready and waiting. Now the fight began.

Marsha charged, kicking and punching. Packo fought his way around the large chamber. Young Sooze, plucky as ever, did much to encourage his timid companions who had become understandably reticent since the whites' boisterous return. Para was particularly venomous in his attempts to beat the enemy. And he was the first brown to fall. At the forefront of the battle he took a savage blow to the side of his head. He staggered and fell. The white then pummelled blows on Para's head as some of the weaker browns stood back in shock.

The whites were strong, and they were beginning to win the day. Marsha and Packo could not overpower them while the browns were being picked off with ease.

'Tunnels, tunnels,' Marsha shouted, his voice cutting through the mayhem.

The browns quickly dispersed. The next ploy had to be put into operation. Marsha would attempt to take as many whites as possible, chasing after him down into the Cavern of Bones. Packo was to pretend to flee. A hoard of smooth, rounded rocks lay scattered at the tunnel entrance. Packo was to roll these down the steep-sloping tunnel. Marsha had identified a niche at the very bottom of the tunnel. He would hide there and allow both the whites and the thundering rocks to pass by. There would be no escape from the Cavern of Bones.

Then, the unforeseen happened. Marsha took a savage blow to the head. His vision darkened, his legs gave way and he collapsed as he passed into oblivion.

'Sooze,' Packo called. The young brown had continued to deal blows to weakened whites while the others fled from the scene. Now he pricked his ears. 'You take my place,' Packo said, 'go!'

Packo stood tall on his hind legs. An aura seemed to surround him. The white who had struck Marsha stopped from following up the blow, sensing something strange.

'You whites,' Packo challenged them, 'prepare to meet your doom.' Then he was gone. He raced to the entrance of the Cavern of Bones and disappeared into it. The whites stared after him silently. Ten remained. Around them lay the bodies of seven browns. 'Hey,' one shouted, 'that's the dungeons he's headed for — he's trapped. He's one of the leaders, we can finish him off. Come on.'

They screamed in delight, made their malicious way to the tunnel entrance and plunged into it.

Sooze watched as the tunnel swallowed them. He raced to the entrance and began to try rolling the rocks down. He pushed at the nearest one. It refused to budge. He tried another, same response. Then he heard the racing footfall above. He would go out fighting, but what would happen to Packo? Those whites would tear him to pieces.

▲▼▲

Packo raced down the sharp incline. He had a head start and that was a comfort. Yet, this was a plan which held dangers. It was bold and might serve to eliminate a good number of whites from the struggle. However, there was always a chance that something could go wrong. As he approached the end of the tunnel, seeing again the area of scattered white bones, the fur rose along the length of his back. He located the niche and pressed himself inside, his brown, tawny coat blending perfectly with the hard, dark rock. He crouched uncomfortably in his hiding place, hardly daring to move. He permitted himself a glance up the long, steep passageway. He could see nothing, but he heard them — the slapping of hurried paw pads against the solid ground. He tucked his head in and pressed harder than ever against the rock. The whites rushed past him into the bone-filled chamber. They eyed it malevolently.

'He's got to be here,' the first one said, 'Let's find him.'

The ten hares began a methodical search. They formed a line and worked their way forward scooping piles of damp white bones and tossing them aside. Packo waited, wondering when the first boulder would smash into the chamber. Moments seemed like hours. Nothing happened.

'Here he is,' a coarse voice called triumphantly. He pulled back half a dozen bones and discovered a brown cowering beneath them. Upon closer examination, however, he realised that all he had found was a hare who had died fairly recently.

'Ah! That's not him,' a gruff-sounding white shouted impatiently. He reached for the fragile body and tossed it back towards the entrance in disgust. 'Come on, he must be here somewhere,'

Now the search took on an air of frenzy. They were tired of this silly game, they wanted action. A white began to sniff his way towards the tunnel, approaching ever nearer Packo's place of concealment. He pricked his ears and hopped forward two paces. He was directly opposite Packo. He turned his head and gazed directly into Packo's eyes.

'Aha!' he shouted, 'come and see what I've . . . .'

A huge rock smashed into his body and sent it crashing back into the chamber. The rock spun wildly into the sea of bones sending them flying violently in every direction. Two of the whites were struck by bones and they howled painfully. Another rock thundered down, then another. The chamber took on a macabre life of its own. The bones began to dance, flung into the air as the speeding boulders plunged into them. The dead had returned to take vengeance on their aggressors. Then, calm returned. There was silence save for the whimpering of the injured. Packo stayed put. The surviving whites raced to the tunnel and charged up it. It was a mistake that they would regret immediately. The second avalanche began. The leading white caught the full brunt of the first boulder. His body slowed its progress slightly and allowed the others to run back into the chamber. The impact also deflected the boulder from its true course and as the whites raced past him Packo glanced out to see the rock ricocheting crazily. He leapt from the niche at the last second. The boulder crashed into it and then chased him into the chamber.

The four remaining whites stared at him. Packo jumped to one side and the boulder careered past him, grinding to a shattering halt at the far side of the chamber. Another thundered in. Packo was as in much danger as the whites. He sought refuge along the side walls. Two enraged whites tried to approach him. Another boulder, then another. There was utter confusion. Shrapnel from the broken bones sprayed everywhere. Packo had nowhere to hide. Either a boulder, a flying piece of bone, or even a white would get him. As the boulders continued to rush into the chamber a new menace threatened. The rocks were now colliding with each other and the enclosed space was showered with razor sharp fragments. There was no escape.

▲▼▲

Sooze looked nervously around him. Who had made the noise overhead? He could not see anything. He put his weight behind one of the boulders. He must try to dispatch at least one, give Packo some sort of chance. He strained hard. Nothing. Figures appeared in the digging area. Sooze squinted but he could not be sure who they were. They raced towards him and he braced himself for the attack.

'Sooze, Sooze, what's going on?'

'Lotto, it's you. Marsha took a blow, Packo rushed down the tunnel, goaded the whites to follow. I can't budge these boulders.'

Lotto tucked his considerable weight behind one of them. It moved easily and set off on its course down the tunnel. Lotto worked away sending another five on their way.

'Now,' he said, 'I'll line these up. We must wait a short while, let the whites think that the onslaught has ceased. Then we'll roll down the rest. I hope Packo's carefully tucked into that niche.'

While Lotto lined up the remaining boulders Crust revived Marsha. He came to, groggy and disorientated.

'Alright me ole son?' Crust asked.

'Awful pain in my head, but I'll do. What's going on?'

Crust told him

'Where's Swengli?' Marsha asked, his senses returning.

'Wonderin' when the next rock's gonna fall on 'is 'ead 'opefully,' Crust replied chuckling.

Lotto was already rolling the remaining boulders down the tunnel. Marsha waited while he completed the task, shuffling anxiously. As soon as Lotto had finished Marsha gave fresh instructions. 'I'm going down to get Packo. Lotto, take Crust and Sooze, try to find the others. They are alone, and probably afraid.

Remember, they were given two possible hideouts to go to. Go to the nearest one first. I'll meet you at the furthest. Let's hope that they managed to get to one or the other. Try to avoid direct confrontation with Swengli's force until we ascertain their number.'

Marsha plunged into the tunnel. Lotto led Crust and Sooze away. They had hardly disappeared when a posse of six whites raced into the upper openings overlooking the digging area. Swengli had split his forces once again.

▲▼▲

Marsha's head ached and he felt dizzy and nauseous. He strode down the tunnel determinedly. He reached the chamber, and the sight that met him shocked him to the core.

The boulders had fragmented and thrown the jagged pieces crazily to both sides. Whites lay crushed, their bodies as scattered as the bone remnants. And there, in the very centre of the chamber, a brown hind leg protruded from beneath a massive rock. Marsha felt the sickness rise from the pit of his stomach. Packo, the Seer, was dead!

▲▼▲

'Let's stay together,' Lotto advised as they left the digging area. 'Be prepared, we might meet a group of whites.'

'Let's go giv 'em 'ell,' Crust said.

They began to run up one of the main tunnels. Two well-concealed hiding places had been chosen in which the browns could seek refuge should they require it. When they had scattered from the digging area some found themselves en route to one, some towards the other. The sanctuaries were high in the mountain, to the north and to the south. The southern sanctuary was nearest to the digging area; it was to this one that Lotto now headed.

Lotto could never travel at full speed through the tunnels. He was too big. He had to crouch slightly and keep his head low so that his back did not scrape the jagged ceiling. Yet, despite his cramped gait, he was able to move surprisingly quickly. They approached the hiding place. It was situated off the main tunnel, left, right, and left again. As Lotto took that final left turn he stopped in his tracks and his heart sank. The bloodied bodies of eight browns filled his line of vision. They had been severely beaten, savaged beyond all recognition. The entrance to the hiding place was undisturbed. They had failed to reach it.

'Too late,' he whispered.

'Blaw-dy 'ell!' Crust gazed at the carnage.

Suddenly there was a movement behind them. They sprang round.

'Lotto, Lotto,' a weak voice called. A brown limped painfully into view from a side passage. It was Erco, one of Lotto's group.

Lotto rushed forward. His fatherly eye roved over Erco's fragile body.

Erco's right ear hung loosely over his eye, his fur was bloodied like the others, and his front teeth were broken. 'Erco, tell us what happened?'

'We had no chance to get into the hiding place,' Erco began, 'about eight of them attacked us. We fought hard, Lotto, we really did. You would have been proud of us. They wanted to take us prisoner, we refused. They caught Linn and dragged him away. They wanted to know where the does and leverets are. I could hear them shouting and slapping him as we tried to fight the others. Eventually I took a blow and collapsed. When I came to they had gone. Everyone else was dead. I hid. I tried to get into the hiding place but I was too weak to move the rocks at the entrance.'

'You've done everything, you could, Erco,' Lotto consoled him. 'We must assume that they've gone for the does and leverets. They must be after hostages.'

'Erco should 'ide 'ere. 'E can't travel,' Crust said. 'Besides, if Marsha and Packo come lookin', 'e can tell 'em where wiv gone.'

'Agreed,' Lotto said. 'Come Erco, we'll settle you in the hiding place. There are supplies of dried grasses in there. Chew them and put the cud on your wounds. Tell Marsha and Packo where we've gone if they come by. If they don't, stay where you are until we return.'

They settled him and carefully camouflaged the entrance. A small gap was left through which he could peep. He would be safe. If any more whites ventured this way they would find the dead browns and automatically assume that the rest had fled.

▲▼▲

Marsha did not dwell long in the Cavern of Bones. The sight of Packo sickened him. This had been his plan, he should have been beneath that boulder. In those brief moments before he died, he wondered, had Packo somehow realised his destiny? After all they had been through how could Packo's life end so anonymously? It was senseless. He turned and began to run up to the digging area. All was quiet there. He immediately ran to the furthest hideout. He sniffed and recognised familiar scents. The browns were here. He approached the concealed entrance.

'Time to move,' Marsha said.

The browns scrambled out. Mush, a lively youth, was first. He was followed by five others.

'Is this all?' Marsha asked, his heart sinking.

'The whites killed some of our group in the digging area,' Mush told him, 'but I'm sure some managed to escape to the other hideout.'

Suddenly, a voice boomed through the low tunnels. 'We've been waiting for you.' A scraggy white stepped into view. 'Take out the leaders and the rest will fall, Swengli told us. You, big mouth, we'll take you out permanently; the rest maimed or able-bodied, we don't care.' The voice was coarse and malicious.

Marsha stared directly at the posse of seven whites confronting him. They had not followed him, rather they had cleverly awaited his arrival.

The snow cover crunched and cracked under their paws and the wind moaned plaintively. Heavy dark clouds hung in the early evening sky. Soon it would snow again. Lotto, Crust, and Sooze hardly noticed.

They picked their way gingerly down the mountain.

They crossed the valley floor to the next mountain. Like all the others in the range it appeared solid and inaccessible. And like the others there was an entry and, inside, an intricate series of tunnels and chambers. This mountain, however, held one major difference from the others: there was but one entrance, and that one entrance was, therefore, the only exit.

The entrance cum exit presented Lotto with a particular problem. It was exceedingly narrow. He had visited the mountain once previously. He had squeezed his way in painfully, and just as painfully squeezed his way out! Now that was the last problem on his mind. He was going in, and that was that.

They climbed a third of the way to the summit. Then they followed a transverse track which led to the hidden entrance. Entry for Lotto was every bit as uncomfortable as the last time. He took a deep breath, held it, and forced himself forward. At one point he felt the jagged rock snag his fur. He pushed hard with his hind legs, battled on earnestly and at last broke into the larger section of tunnel two feet inside the mountain. The thought struck him that he would not want to have to leave in a hurry.

'If I was Swengli,' Lotto turned and spoke to the others, 'I'd round up all the does and leverets. That way they'd all be accessible and could be used against us, probably by threatening to kill them. If he has arrived here already he'll have them gathered in that large chamber further in. So, this is what we'll do . . .' Lotto outlined his plan.

Crust shook his head. 'It's dead risky, Lotto mate.'

'I know, but the time has come to take a few risks. We don't know how many whites are roaming around. We cannot allow Swengli to hold the does and leverets. We must try to get them out. Besides,' and now he chuckled, 'I have a contingency plan, just in case.' He told Crust no more.

They ran on silently, heading towards the largest chamber. Lotto slowed as they reached their destination. The does and leverets had been gathered just as Lotto had predicted and they now cowered against one of the chamber walls. The whites were sitting around. Swengli was talking.

'You five stay here, don't let anyone near this lot. I'll take the other six and see if we can't call a meeting. Either they all surrender or we will begin to kill the leverets. That should make them sit up!'

Swengli smiled. It was a simple, evil plan; one guaranteed to deliver.

'Now,' Lotto whispered, 'while they are all together.' The time had come for the risky part of his plan.

Lotto burst into the chamber. He ran heavily into the nearest group of whites. He trampled on one, kicked another, stung a third with a short, straight forepaw to the snout, and head butted a fourth sending him crashing against a wall. Simultaneously Crust raced round the outer right hand side and attacked from the rear, nimbly dealing telling blows in sensitive areas. His was a rare breed, the urban hare well practised in his own art of fighting, mean and dirty.

While this initial attack broke out Sooze was leading the bewildered does and leverets out by means of a tunnel at the far end of the chamber. There were eighteen leverets, half of them tiny, and four does. Two of the does accompanied Sooze while two remained to join the fray. Their aggression, so long held back for the sake of their young, was now given full vent. Their presence gave Lotto and Crust an added impetus. Perhaps Lotto's bold plan might yet succeed.

Swengli now showed his leadership qualities. He quickly reorganised the whites after the shock of the initial attack. He kept himself away from the action but continually barked out orders and the whites responded, showing why they had been chosen to become members of the much feared and vaunted terror squad. They formed a solid phalanx which Swengli controlled from the centre. While they did remain trapped as the four hares sought openings to get at them, they protected each other in such a way that a lot of damage could not be inflicted. Lotto realised that no outright victory could be gained here. Phase one of his plan had been successful, the hostages had been freed and by now should be approaching the final tunnel to take them to the exit.

'Retreat,' he called. The does did not understand what he intended and continued to dash around the group of whites. Stoli was there in the thick of the action. She had seen the Seer, she knew what she must do. Suddenly she received a severe blow to the top of the head. Before she collapsed she was dragged into the centre of the phalanx and bitten so savagely that the whites' fur showed crimson. It was a sickening act of thuggery which had the desired effect on the other doe. She shrank back, shocked. Lotto turned to her.

'Go with Crust,' he ordered sharply, 'now.'

She stumbled to the tunnel and Crust took her down it. 'Join the uvers at the exit,' he said gently. 'Go now, yer was great in there.' She looked at him briefly and fled.

Lotto was already retreating. The whites had broken ranks and were rushing towards him. Crust raced past Lotto and struck a smart punch to the leading white's jaw. Lotto picked up the body and threw it into the advancing whites. A few precious seconds had been gained. They ran down the tunnel without looking back. When they arrived at the wider section of tunnel just inside the exit they found it congested with does and leverets.

'Only just got here,' Sooze called out.

Crust searched the ground and found two decent sized rocks. He rolled them forward and waited.

The leverets began to file out. Half of them had gone when Crust picked up the first rock and rifled it straight and true into the tunnel. A scream, chill and frightening, reverberated through the passageways. Crust waited five seconds and then drilled the other rock through the tunnel. No sound this time. The whites had gone to ground.

'Crust, you go with them, get the leverets and does to the hiding place with Erco.'

'We'll never make it, Lotto mate. Them whites will be 'ere soon.'

'My contingency plan!' Lotto smiled. 'I'll detain the whites here. They can't get past me if I stand in the tunnel.'

''Ow will yer get out?'

'Don't worry about that, just get the youngsters to safety.'

The whites, hearing the voices, began to creep forward. One pounced. He caught Lotto by surprise and sank his teeth into one of his ears. Lotto felt the pain shoot through his body. Crust thumped the white in the larynx, forcing him to release his grip. He followed up immediately with a straight jab to the snout. The white passed out.

'Go Crust, please. I'll look after the situation here.'

'Yeah, I know,' Crust replied, 'watch yerself mate.'

As soon as Crust had disappeared Lotto backed into the tunnel. He wedged himself inside, feeling the walls pinch his flanks. Nobody else was getting out!

Some moments passed. A white crept forward, took one look at Lotto, and called back, 'One left.'

The others entered the widened tunnel. Eight of them. The numbers had been reduced. Swengli brought up the rear. 'Ah!' he said as he appraised the situation. 'You hope to detain us here.'

Lotto gave no reply.

'You won't detain us long,' Swengli said smugly. 'These are not ordinary hares you see before you, these are elite fighters. Any one of us could take you out in one to one combat. Choose one of us. Let this war be decided by the outcome of that fight. Winner takes all. You win, the rest of us leave.'

Lotto maintained his silence. He watched Swengli closely. He was motivating his troops, giving them confidence. And all the time his eyes were flashing, searching eagerly for some way out.

Lotto remained firmly entrenched.

Swengli appreciated that he was not going to succeed in tempting Lotto to move. There was only one way that would be achieved. He inclined his head to his right. A white charged forward, parried Lotto's first blow and bit deeply into a forepaw. Lotto grimaced and immediately struck the hare with his free paw. The white released his grip and backed off. The damage had been done. Blood spurted from Lotto's wound. He was afforded little time to dwell on his injury. Another replaced the attacker who had stumbled away. Lotto squeezed back. He was very firmly wedged now. The white snapped and snarled trying feverishly to reach the one good paw. Lotto responded by guiding it astutely, hitting his target several times before the white was forced to retreat. Then another white tried, then another. Lotto continued to lose blood and as it flowed so too did his energy. The whites maintained their barrage of attacks. They saw him weakening and knew that all they had to do was to keep him occupied.

Lotto began to wonder what it was all about. He had spent almost his entire life as a bully, lording it over any weaker than himself. Now, he was defending the weak against bullies. He smiled. Whoever would have thought such a transformation possible? In this one act of selflessness he had vindicated his life. There was something special about that.

Another attack came. The white jumped at him. What was going on? Then he felt the teeth sink into his throat, felt the pain and nausea, felt the darkness descend. His jugular had been ripped open. He was dying. He was out of it now. Yet, there was one more contribution he would make. Summoning his rapidly declining strength he pressed himself awkwardly against the walls of the narrow tunnel. The whites would have great difficulty removing the body of this magnificent hare.

Marsha eyed his enemies with disdain. Their kind had been

responsible for Packo's death, they had slaughtered innocent browns, perhaps even now Lotto and Crust were at their mercy. As his anger erupted he screamed, 'No more slavery, no more.' He tore into the whites venomously. He had abhorred violence all his life and yet now, at this moment of his existence, he could not stand by. He would match violence with violence.

'Come on, lads,' the young Mush shouted, taking his lead from Marsha, 'slavery no more.' The browns, following Marsha's example, tore into the whites. Utter confusion followed. The whites had not expected any serious opposition. Mush led the browns trading smart blows.

'I'll never dig for you lot again,' Mush shouted, 'never.'

His infectiousness spread. Four whites lay dead before the remaining three fled. Mush wanted to follow them, to finish them off. Marsha stopped him. 'We've made our point,' he told him. 'Thank you all, you were amazing, every one of you.'

The browns cheered. They had suffered only minor injuries. An important psychological battle had been won, the browns were buoyant. 'We must go to the other hiding place,' Marsha said, 'we need to join forces.'

As soon as he arrived there he realised the worst. The buoyancy in the group ebbed as they gazed on the dead, mutilated bodies of their friends. It was clear to everyone that a new terror squad was abroad.

'Hello! ... Hello!'

The voice was faint but clear.

Marsha turned to the blocked hiding place.

'Who is there?' he asked.

'It's me, Erco.'

Marsha removed a boulder and peered in. He was shocked by the sight of the suffering hare. He could see where Erco had attempted to place cud on his wounds but had failed to find the right spots. The wounds were bleeding still and his mouth was bloodied where his teeth had been smashed. Marsha quickly set to patching him up while Erco struggled to talk.

'Swengli . . . gone for the does and leverets . . . Lotto after him

. . . long time . . . should be . . .'

'All right, all right,' Marsha tried to soothe him.

Suddenly there was a shuffling sound further up the tunnel.

'Someone coming,' Mush whispered.

'In here,' Marsha ordered. 'Block it up. I'll challenge them and lead them away, I'll be back when I can.'

Marsha concealed himself in a niche and stood waiting, ready to pounce. He could strike and be off. The footfall, slow and ponderous, approached. Then it stopped. Whoever it was was sniffing at the entrance to the hiding place. Marsha could not allow them to discover that the browns were there. He jumped out, drew back a forepaw, and stopped in mid-air. Sooze stood before him, terrified. Behind Sooze the leverets came into view, three does helping them along. Finally Crust appeared.

'Cor blimey, Marsha, glad t' see yer. It's blawdy cold out there.'

'Where's Lotto?'

''oldin' up Swengli an' company so we could get away.'

'How long did it take you to get here, Crust?'

'Ages mate. We 'ad t' keep stoppin', these little lads can't run too far, bless 'em. Lotto should be well on 'is way by naw.'

It was then that they heard the noise further up the tunnel.

''Ere 'e is, right on time.'

Crust turned and a racing white, his mouth bloodied, struck him ferociously. He was out cold. Marsha battled bravely, but he was alone. The does were exhausted, the leverets petrified, the remaining browns trapped in the hiding place. Marsha took out two whites before being winded and pinned down by three others. Swengli stepped forward and gloated.

'Ah! One of the leaders I presume.' He bit savagely into Marsha's hind leg. The bone fractured. Marsha grimaced as pain exploded through his body. Swengli struck out with a mighty forepaw punch directly to Marsha's left eye. He passed out.

'Right lads, take them all down to our quarters, this rebellion is over.'

Chapter Twenty-One

While Swengli's troops led the defeated browns down to their quarters another drama was continuing deep within the mountain. Unknown to Marsha, Packo had survived, he was still alive.

When Packo had run into the Cavern of Bones he knew that he was in real peril. The whites were no danger to him. They were too busy trying to avoid the crashing rocks and ricocheting bones. This was their shared peril. He tried to make his way back from the side wall to the centre. He hoped that there he might avoid the boulders if he could see them coming. He found himself standing over the dead brown he had discovered on his first visit to the Cavern of Bones, the one whose body had been disturbed by the whites. Then another boulder was trundling down, gathering momentum as it reached its goal. Packo turned and jumped towards the rear of the chamber. He rotated his eyes. There was but one thing he could do. He plunged into the black water which formed a small pool directly opposite the entrance to the chamber. It was icy cold. As he swam down the sides converged, leading into a tunnel. The boulder crashed into the water above him and settled on the narrow tunnel entrance. He was trapped.

He attempted vainly to push back the boulder. No chance. He began to swim through the narrow water-filled tunnel. As he swam it became narrower and narrower. Would it become too narrow for him to pass through? He concentrated on remaining calm. Marsha had introduced him to water, had been his mentor. He must not panic, he must remain calm, conserve energy, release a little air occasionally.

Yet, he could not hold his breath forever and, although he fought his rising panic, he quickened his stroke. There was no way back. Was there a way forward?

His heart began to pound, his lungs began to scream. The tunnel walls pressed close against him and began to confine his movements. He wriggled and squirmed on and on. His heart thudded, his lungs were on the verge of explosion. Would the tunnel ever end? Suddenly, the tunnel turned vertically. Up and up and up.

He broke through the surface, coughing and gasping for breath. He paddled his forepaws frantically as he slipped back below the water line. He re-emerged, spluttering. Then his paws felt firm ground beneath him. He forced himself forward and collapsed, exhausted, on dry ground. He had made it. Someone was looking after him. He thought of his mother. Waves of nausea flooded over him. His lungs could hardly take the air in quickly enough. He rose to his feet, arched his body, and suffered the agony. It was several minutes before he began to return to normal. He lay down and rested.

He awoke from a short sleep, confused. Where was he? How had he got here? He lay still as the pieces of his memory gradually fitted together to form a complete picture. How were his friends? Had he slept for long? What must he do to get out? He began to explore the chamber.

It was ten paces across, six wide. The black water skirted one side, solid rock the other three. No exit. He tried to touch the ceiling, it was beyond his reach. He examined it minutely. It was black, all black. He was trapped yet again. Perhaps he could swim through the black water again, push the boulder out. He doubted that he could. If he tried and did not succeed he would not be able to swim back again. He was in a grave.

Weariness overtook him. Try as he might he could not keep his eyes open. Perhaps he might sleep, just a short nap. The words came to him. 'You're special, Packo, find your destiny.'

He awoke abruptly, the words repeating in his mind, 'find your destiny'. Those words had come back to haunt him so many times, so many times he had wished that he might learn what he must do.

He glanced around. At the far end of the chamber a narrow shaft of pale light gleamed against the chamber wall. Daylight! He ran over and peered up. Two paces from the wall a steep tunnel broke through the ceiling. And the tunnel itself was a wondrous sight. Myriad colours glistened and laser-like beams criss-crossed producing a wealth of intricate patterns filled with delicate shades. This was the very centre of the mountain and here an abundance of ice rocks shone, reflecting the light which burst into the tunnel when the sun was at its zenith.

Slowly, the inspiration he had sought for so very long dawned upon him. Packo knew what he must do, knew now how to confront his destiny. Life had to do with giving, and in giving all he would find his real self. His mind was absolutely lucid.

He jumped up, shooting through the narrow tunnel opening. He landed and immediately began to slip back. The tunnel was even steeper than he had gauged. However, the ice rocks jutting out from the walls provided adequate purchase. Keeping three paw contact at all times he began to climb methodically, carefully, with grim determination. Progress was slow. He paused occasionally to glance towards the pin prick of light high above. He did not allow himself to become despondent. He knew with a clarity never previously experienced that he would achieve his objective. One way or another he would be free. Behind him the tunnel became dark, black and forbidding as his body blocked the light. It was as if he was entering a new phase of existence. This tunnel was leading him to the final encounter. He was ready.

He climbed on, clutching the ice rocks, the objects of despotism his means of freedom. Then he spotted a side tunnel. He fell into it and gathered his breath. 'Two rights and a left.' He knew the ancient instruction. He set off and finally emerged into the open air. Snow covered the mountain but here and there spikes of greenery broke through, the first signs of spring. It was an apt reminder that even throughout winter's deathly stranglehold, life waited quietly to re-emerge.

He inhaled the cold air and filled his lungs. It was clean and crisp. He paused, surveyed the scene, and then began his descent. Suddenly, running by his side, was the old hare, the Purveyor.

'Well, Packo, you know what to do?'

'Yes,' Packo replied, 'I know.'

'No doubts?'

'No doubts,' he answered simply.

'In time wisdom is given to you, but the choice to act on that wisdom is yours. You do appreciate that?'

Packo smiled wistfully. 'I was prepared a long time ago; it was only the knowledge I lacked. You know that, you were once a Seer.'

It was the old hare's turn to smile. 'You know then?'

'Yes, now I know.'

Packo continued. The old hare had vanished. Packo did not bother to look for him. He knew already.

Chapter Twenty-Two

'You might yet decide not to co-operate. Let me end any lingering doubts you might have.'

Swengli eyed his prisoners malevolently. They were herded into the whites' quarters and set against the far wall. Swengli's terror squad stood by menacingly, joined by the other surviving whites, eleven in all.

'Eyes!' Swengli shouted.

Three whites stepped forward. The others stood back, ready to pounce if anyone made a break for freedom. The browns' eyes were gritted. Two held a brown on either side and forced him to open his eyes while the one in front kicked a shower of tiny rock particles into the frightened face. Crust looked on in disgust. Marsha, at his side, seemed hardly aware of what was happening. The pain from his shattered hind leg racked his body. He was completely blind in the eye Swengli had savaged and the dragging to the whites' quarters had totally exhausted him. When they came to Marsha the whites looked to Swengli.

'Leave him,' Swengli ordered, 'I shall kill him soon enough.'

Crust had not been identified as a stranger. The fact that he was such a skinny creature probably made the whites think that he was as docile as the other browns. Two whites grabbed him and he adopted a submissive stance; eyes wide and frightened. As the grit was kicked he closed his eyes ensuring that most stayed out. Then he lowered his head and howled as the others had done. The whites moved on while he blinked away the small amount of grit that had penetrated. He was ready to act when the opportunity arose.

'Now,' Swengli announced as the gritting was complete, 'listen to me, all of you. You cannot hope, ever, to beat a superior race. You were born to serve, and believe me, serve you shall. I want you to know exactly what happens to rabble rousers. Bring him forward.'

He pointed to Marsha. Two whites bit into the flesh at either side of his neck and dragged him forward roughly. Not a sound came from him. His broken hind leg trailed after him. He lay in a heap before Swengli. Suddenly Swengli struck a massive blow to Marsha's rib cage. Fresh pain exploded throughout his body as he lapsed into unconsciousness. Swengli raised his paw to deliver the final blow, the blow to end this futile insurrection.

Crust could stand by no longer. Better to die in one last act of defiance than to watch this brutal murder. He stepped forward.

'Fink yer brave, don't yer?'

Swengli stopped in mid swing.

'Yeah, you, maggot 'ead. Om talkin' t' yer.'

Swengli lowered his paw. 'You may have made mistakes before, brown, but you'll never make another. Take him.'

Crust was ready, the street fighter against assassins. Before the whites could move a shriek echoed within the chamber. Instinctively all looked up. Packo erupted from the food tunnel. He flew through the air and landed squarely in front of Swengli.

'This,' he shouted, 'is between me and him.' His voice carried a powerful authority. No one moved, not even Swengli.

Crust stared. Marsha had whispered to him when they had first arrived in the whites' quarters that Packo was dead, that there was no hope. But here he was, here he was. There was something different about him, something had changed.

All the browns pricked their ears. Hope had come. This thought flashed through their minds like a light in the darkness. Something exciting was afoot.

Swengli stood and took stock. He could call his terror squad, order them to rip this upstart to pieces. But now the onus lay with him. He must tackle this brown, and in overcoming this one, his power over browns and whites alike would be absolute.

'Stand back,' he commanded. 'This I shall do personally.'

His pride, bristling and assertive, reared its ugly head. Packo had anticipated as much. Now came the test, one to one combat.

The two hares eyed one another. Swengli's gaze was sinister and sardonic; Packo's calm and fearless. So the contest began, a struggle for nerve. Packo recognised it for what it was. Swengli smiled. Packo was slightly bigger than him but he had never yet met a brown he couldn't bully, couldn't make cringe. Why should this one be any different?

Crust, the other browns, and even the whites, stood by, mesmerised. The whites recognised the determination in this brown. He had something about him that they had not encountered before, an aloofness they did not associate with browns. Swengli was completely unaware of it.

'You dare to threaten me,' Swengli spoke softly. 'I have killed browns for looking at me, and the killing has been slow and painful. Yours will be the same.'

Packo refused to be drawn. In response to Swengli's hate stare, Packo's was level-tempered.

Suddenly Swengli struck. He rushed forward, front paws flailing. Packo protected himself, covering his head with his forepaws, taking the barrage of blows and holding his ground. Swengli broke off and moved slightly backwards, puzzlement in his eyes. But Packo allowed him no time to reflect. He struck. He slapped Swengli with a right, then jabbed with his left to the snout. A trickle of blood emerged. Swengli was furious. He leapt forward attempting to smother Packo. Packo reacted by nimbly breaking to his left. He delivered a telling blow to Swengli's throat, and immediately brought a paw down heavily on Swengli's head, turned and aimed an almighty kick to the left flank. Swengli breathed hard as the air was forced from his body. Packo was back again. He bit Swengli's left hind leg, felt his teeth jar on the bone, and broke away. Swengli swore and made to turn. He keeled over. Packo surged forward pummelling blows on Swengli's head. He stood back momentarily and then, as Swengli foolishly looked up, struck another punch into his larynx. Packo turned before Swengli realised what was happening and placed another kick into the rib cage, shattering three bones.

Swengli lay still, his breathing was coarse, his heart exploding, his left hind leg oozing blood. Summoning his remaining breath he shouted hoarsely, 'Kill, kill.' He dropped his head for the last time.

Whites swarmed forward. Four tore at Packo. He punched, kicked, bit, punched again. The wave of whites rushed on.

'Cam on lads, give 'em wot for!' Crust raced into the attack, a one-hare terror squad. The other browns threw themselves in, crazy with pain, fighting now with a glimmer of hope and a common determination. Slavery no more, no more.

The whites were experienced and strong. They refused to panic. Packo was deluged beneath three of them. He was pinned down and blow upon blow rained upon him. Crust, nimble and agile as ever, could not be caught. He tried valiantly to reach Packo but every path was immediately cut off by another white or a brown suffering a beating. Finally, he began to tire. The browns, the surviving three does and the older leverets, fought courageously. They were no match, however, for this fighting force. Inexorably they were beaten into submission. Crust continued to dash around offering assistance wherever he could, and, although he did not despair, he came to realise that it was only a matter of time until defeat came. The browns were being brushed aside like fallen autumn leaves. The end was near.

Marsha lay in a heap. The battle raging about him bit dully into his semi-consciousness. He was unable to react. Whatever was happening was beyond his control. Yet, somehow he began to appreciate that the whites were being quelled. Delusions! So near to death he had been permitted his final dream. He could hardly see, yet, whites were fighting whites! Crazy, the whole fracas was crazy! Then the noise began to subside. He had failed. Dark forgetfulness enveloped him.

Chapter Twenty-Three

'Shake a leg, Marsha, me ole son, shake a leg!'

'Take it easy, Crust, take it easy.'

They were approaching the tunnel exit. Ahead a ray of soft warm sunlight greeted them. Marsha was shuffling along as best he could. His hind leg had healed but it was now permanently crooked. He still felt the odd twinge of pain in his ribs, but they were healing nicely. Now, as he neared the first natural light he had seen for many weeks, he had to blink away the water from his one remaining good eye. He felt the air on his snout. It was crisp, fresh, and inviting. He was eager to breathe it deeply after the long, dark period of his convalescence.

Then he emerged into the sunlight. Its warmth, combining with the cooling breeze, exhilarated him. He gazed out towards the horizon. How strange it was to see with only one eye! He had to turn his head in order to look all around. It was a glorious sight. A deep sea of undulating purple swayed gently. The winter had long gone and spring had transformed the land into a wonderful summer of heathered valleys and mountains of grassy lower slopes and sun-sparkled shale summits. Clouds cast shadows across the landscape changing the hues and deepening the colours. There was a vibrancy in the air, and it was infectious.

''Ow's the leg?' Crust asked.

'Well, I'll never chase the wind again,' Marsha smiled wryly, 'but there's no pain.'

'No pain.' Crust repeated the words thoughtfully.

'A different type of pain we both feel, Crust. In time we will learn to live with it.'

Crust's thoughts drifted back. He had replayed them so very many times. They always began at exactly the same instant. Packo was off to his left, buried by whites. Crust himself was fighting frantically and the other browns were giving everything, yet they could not hope to overcome such powerful adversaries. Not only was the battle lost, the war was too.

It was then that a most astonishing thing happened. A small group of whites appeared. Their leader, whom Crust later discovered to be named Caena, surveyed the scene briefly, then ordered his followers into action. They attacked their own kind and it was their intervention that won the day. They admitted subsequently that they could not have overcome the bullying whites without the great efforts of the browns.

Swengli was dead. Packo had seen to that before he had been engulfed. The newly arrived whites gathered around Swengli's body. 'He has dictated to us about ice rocks for too long,' Caena announced. 'Our elders listened to him. We, the younger generation, have rejected his despotism, we are not all as evil as he and his killer squads. We have come to help.'

The leverets had come through unscathed. Most had been too young and too frightened to understand what was happening and had cowered in a corner. Only two does and three bucks had survived, all badly injured. A new community would eventually evolve. Packo had been beaten to death, but Marsha was clinging tenaciously to life. Only Crust, of all the browns, had avoided any serious injury.

Crust took Packo's broken body to the Cavern of Bones and there laid him to rest. It seemed fitting that his final resting place should be amongst the ancestors of those for whom he had given his life. Crust had then gone to search for Lotto. His life had been sacrificed for the very weakest of all the browns. His would be a place of great honour whenever the tale was told. Crust sealed the entrance to the tunnel; it was all he could think of doing.

The whites who rescued them seemed a different breed from those who had cast the deep shadow. They nursed the injured back to health, adept at using the natural remedies that grew in abundance as spring arrived. They tended Marsha day and night, applied a splint to his broken leg, and tenderly cleaned his wounds. They gathered fresh food and distributed.it. When the browns were able to fend for themselves, the whites returned to their homeland.

'So, Marsha,' Crust said, breaking the silence into which they had fallen, 'wot now?'

'For me, Crust, I shall stay. The remainder of my life will be spent helping these hares to rediscover themselves.'

'Yeah,' Crust nodded, 'that's good.'

'And you, Crust, you will leave, be off again in search of adventure.'

'Adventure! Nah, not adventure. Om goin' t' look for meself, like wot Packo was doin'. 'E's dead: the quest 'as bin passed on.'

A huge smile broke across Marsha's face. 'Long live the quest.'

'Yeah,' Crust smiled back, 'long live the quest.'

'The end of life is but a beginning. Those who have confronted fear, who have searched long and given everything, move on. Some, those special few, remain behind in a new form. They are the silent running companions, those who at times exhort and suggest. These are the Purveyors who know what the struggle is all about, for they have answered the call with their lives.

Every day we are asked to answer the call. Will you answer it, today?'

Prophecy of Tuarug: Last extant verses.